Hey Nostradamus!

GOD IS NOWHERE GOD IS NOW HERE
GOD IS NOWHERE GOD IS NOW HERE

Pregnant and secretly married, Cheryl Anway scribbles her last will and testament – and eerie premonition – on a school binder shortly before a rampaging trio of misfit classmates gun her down in a high-school cafeteria. Overrun with paranoia, teenage angst and religious zeal in the ensuing massacre's wake, this sleepy Vancouver neighbourhood declares its saints, brands its demons and finally moves on.

But for a handful of people still reeling from that horrific day, life remains perpetually derailed. Four dramatically different characters tell their stories in their own words: Cheryl, who calmly narrates her own death; Jason, the boy no one knew was her husband, still marooned ten years later by his loss; Heather, the woman trying to love the shattered Jason; and Jason's father Reg, a cruelly religious man no one suspects is still worth loving. Each wrestles with God, self-defeat and a crippling inability to hold on to those they love.

Coupland's most surprising and soulful novel yet, rich with his trademark cultural acuity and dark humour, *Hey Nostradamus!* ties themes of alienation, violence and misguided faith into a fateful and unforgettable knot from which four people must untangle their lives.

Also by Douglas Coupland

Fiction:

Generation X

Shampoo Planet

Life After God

Microserfs

Girlfriend in a Coma

Miss Wyoming

All Families Are Psychotic

Non-fiction:

Polaroids from the Dead

City of Glass

Souvenir of Canada

God Hates Japan [only available in Japanese]

Hey Nostradamus!

Douglas Coupland

Flamingo
An Imprint of HarperCollins*Publishers*

Flamingo
An Imprint of HarperCollins*Publishers*
77–85 Fulham Palace Road,
Hammersmith, London W6 8JB

Flamingo is a registered trade mark of
HarperCollins*Publishers* Limited

www.heynostradamus.com

www.coupland.com

Published by Flamingo 2003
    3 5 7 9 8 6 4

First published in the USA by Bloomsbury US 2003, and in
Canada by RandomHouse Canada 2003

Copyright © Douglas Coupland 2003

Douglas Coupland asserts the moral right to
be identified as the author of this work

A catalogue record for this book
is available from the British Library

ISBN 0 00 716250 2

Set in Sabon and Helvetica

Printed and bound in Great Britain by
Clays Ltd, St Ives plc

Behold, I tell you a mystery;
we shall not all sleep, but we shall all be changed,
in a moment, in the twinkling of an eye, at the last trumpet;
for the trumpet will sound, and the dead will be raised imperishable,
and we shall be changed.

I Cor. 15:51–52

Contents

Part One

1988: Cheryl

I believe that what separates humanity from everything else in this world – spaghetti, binder paper, deep-sea creatures, edelweiss and Mount McKinley – is that humanity alone has the capacity at any given moment to commit all possible sins. Even those of us who try to live a good and true life remain as far away from grace as the Hillside Strangler or any demon who ever tried to poison the village well. What happened that morning only confirms this.

It was a glorious fall morning. The sun burned a girly pink over the mountain ranges to the west, and the city had yet to generate its daily smog blanket. Before driving to school in my little white Chevette, I went into the living room and used my father's telescope to look down at the harbor, as smooth as mercury, and on its surface I could see the moon dimming over East Vancouver. And then I looked up into the real sky and saw the moon on the cusp of being over-powered by the sun.

My parents had already gone to work, and my brother, Chris, had left for swim team hours before. The house was quiet – not even a clock ticking – and as I opened the front door, I looked back and saw some gloves and unopened letters on the front hallway desk. Beyond them, on the living room's gold carpet, were some discount warehouse sofas and a lamp on a side table that we never used because the light bulb always popped when we switched it on. It was lovely, all that silence and all that calm order, and I thought how lucky I was to have had a good home. And then I turned and walked outside. I was already a bit late, but I was in no hurry.

Normally I used the garage door, but today I wanted a touch of formality. I had thought that this morning would be my last truly innocent glance at my childhood home – not because of what really ended up happening, but because of another, smaller drama that was supposed to have unfolded.

I'm glad that the day was as quiet and as average as it was. The air was see-your-breath chilly, and the front lawn was crunchy with frost, as though each blade had been batter fried. The brilliant blue and black Steller's jays were raucous and clearly up to no good on the eaves trough, and because of the frost, the leaves on the Japanese maples had been converted into stained-glass shards. The world was unbearably pretty, and it continued being so all the way down the mountain to school. I felt slightly high because of the beauty, and the inside of my head tickled. I wondered if this is how artists go through life, with all of its sensations tickling their craniums like a peacock feather.

*   *   *

I was the last to park in the school's lot. That's always such an uneasy feeling no matter how together you think you are – being the last person there, wherever *there* may be.

I was carrying four large binders and some textbooks, and

when I tried shutting the Chevette's door, it wouldn't close properly. I tried slamming it with my hip, but that didn't work; it only made the books spray all over the pavement. But I didn't get upset.

Inside the school, classes were already in session and the hallways were as silent as the inside of my house, and I thought to myself, *What a day for silence.*

I needed to go to my locker before class, and as I was working my combination lock, Jason came up from behind.

"Boo."

"Jason – don't do that. Why aren't you in class?"

"I saw you parking, so I left."

"You just walked out?"

"Forget about that, Miss Priss. Why were you being so weird on the phone last night?"

"I was being weird?"

"Jesus, Cheryl – don't act like your airhead friends."

"Anything else?"

"Yes. You're my wife, so act like it."

"How should I be acting, then?"

"Cheryl, look: in God's eyes we're not two individuals, okay? We're one unit now. So if you dick around with me, then you're only dicking around with yourself."

And Jason was right. We were married – had been for about six weeks at that point – but we were the only ones who knew it.

*   *   *

I was late for school because I'd wanted everyone out of the house before I used a home pregnancy test. I was quite calm about it – I was a married woman, and shame wasn't a factor. My period was three weeks late, and facts were facts.

Instead of the downstairs bathroom I shared with my brother, I used the guest bathroom upstairs. The guest bathroom felt one notch more medical, one notch less tinged by personal history – less accusatory, to be honest. And the olive fixtures and foil wallpaper patterned with brown bamboo looked swampy and dank when compared to the test's scientific white-and-blue box. And there's not much more to say, except that fifteen minutes later I was officially pregnant and I was late for math class.

* * *

"Jesus, Cheryl . . ."

"Jason, don't curse. You can swear, but don't curse."

"Pregnant?"

I was quiet.

"You're sure?"

"I'm late for math class. Aren't you even happy?"

A student walked by, maybe en route to see the principal.

Jason squinted like he had dust in his eyes. "Yeah – well, of course – sure I am."

I said, "Let's talk about it at homeroom break."

"I can't. I'm helping Coach do setup for the Junior A team. I promised him ages ago. Lunchtime then. In the cafeteria."

I kissed him on his forehead. It was soft, like antlers I'd once touched on a petting zoo buck. "Okay. I'll see you there."

He kissed me in return and I went to math class.

* * *

I was on the yearbook staff, so I can be precise here. Delbrook Senior Secondary is a school of 1,106 students located about a five-minute walk north of the Trans-Canada

Highway, up the algae-green slope of Vancouver's North Shore. It opened in the fall of 1962, and by 1988, my senior year, its graduates numbered about thirty-four thousand. During high school, most of them were nice enough kids who'd mow lawns and baby-sit and get drunk on Friday nights and maybe wreck a car or smash a fist through a basement wall, not even knowing why they'd done it, only that it had to happen. Most of them grew up in rectangular postwar homes that by 1988 were called tear-downs by the local real estate agents. Nice lots. Nice trees and vines. Nice views.

As far as I could tell, Jason and I were the only married students ever to have attended Delbrook. It wasn't a neighborhood that married young. It was neither religious nor irreligious, although back in eleventh-grade English class I did a tally of the twenty-six students therein: five abortions, three dope dealers, two total sluts, and one perpetual juvenile delinquent. I think that's what softened me up for conversion: I didn't want to inhabit that kind of moral world. Was I a snob? Was I a hypocrite? And who was *I* to even judge? Truth be told, I wanted everything those kids had, but I wanted it by playing the game correctly. This meant legally and religiously and – this is the part that was maybe wrong – I wanted to outsmart the world. I had, and continue to have, a nagging suspicion that I used the system simply to get what I wanted. Religion included. Does that cancel out whatever goodness I might have inside me?

Jason was right: *Miss Priss*.

* * *

Math class was x's and y's and I felt trapped inside a repeating dream, staring at these two evil little letters who tormented me with their constant need to balance and be equal with each other. They should just get married and form a new letter together and put an end to all the nonsense. And then they should have kids.

I thought about my own child-to-be as I stared out the window, turning the pages only when I heard everybody else turn theirs. I saw fleeting images of breast-feeding, prams and difficult labor, my knowledge of motherhood being confined mostly to magazines and cartoons. I ignored Lauren Hanley, two rows over, who held a note in her hand that she obviously wanted me to read. Lauren was one of the few people left from my *Youth Alive!* group who would still speak to me after rumors began spreading that Jason and I were making it.

Carol Schraeger passed the note my way; it was a plea from Lauren to talk during homeroom break. We did, out by her locker. I know Lauren saw this meeting as being charged with drama, and my serenity must have bothered her.

"Everyone's talking, Cheryl. Your reputation is being tarnished. You have to do something about it."

Lauren was probably the key blabber, but I was a married woman, so why should I care? I said, "Let people say what they want, Lauren. I take comfort in knowing that my best friends are squelching any rumors from the start, right?"

She reddened. "But everyone *knows* your Chevette was parked at Jason's all weekend while his parents were away in the Okanogan."

"So?"

"So you guys could have been doing anything in there – not that you were – but imagine what it looked like."

Truth was, Jason and I *were* doing everything in there that weekend, but I have to admit that for a moment or two I enjoyed watching Lauren squirm at my nonresponse. In any event, I was far too preoccupied to have any sort of conversation. I told Lauren I had to go to my homeroom and sequence some index cards for an oral presentation later that afternoon on early Canadian fur trappers, and I left.

In homeroom I sat at my desk and wrote over and over on my pale blue binder the words GOD IS NOWHERE/GOD IS NOW HERE/GOD IS NOWHERE/GOD IS NOW HERE. When this binder with these words was found, caked in my evaporating blood, people made a big fuss about it, and when my body is shortly lowered down into the planet, these same words will be felt-penned all over the surface of my white coffin. But all I was doing was trying to clear out my head and think of nothing, to generate enough silence to make time stand still.

*   *   *

Stillness is what I have here now – wherever *here* is. I'm no longer a part of the world and I'm still not yet a part of what follows. I think there are others from the shooting here with me, but I can't tell where. And for whatever it's worth, I'm no longer pregnant, and I have no idea what that means. Where's my baby? What happened to it? How can it just go away like that?

It's quiet here – quiet like my parents' house, and quiet in the way I wanted silence when writing on my binder. The only sounds I can hear are prayers and curses; they're the only sounds with the power to cross over to where I am.

I can only hear the words of these prayers and curses – not the voice of the speaker. I'd like to hear from Jason and my family, but I'm unable to sift them out.

Dear God,
Remove the blood from the souls of these young men
and women. Strip their memories of our human vile-
ness. Return them to the Garden and make them babes,
make them innocent. Erase their memories of today.

As I'm never going to be old, I'm glad that I never lost my
sense of wonder about the world, although I have a hunch it
would have happened pretty soon. I loved the world, its
beauty and bigness as well as its smallness: the first thirty
seconds of the Beatles' "Lovely Rita"; pigeons sitting a fist
apart on the light posts entering Stanley Park; huckleberries
both bright orange and dusty blue the first week of June;
powdered snow down to the middle gondola tower of
Grouse Mountain by the third week of every October;
grilled-cheese sandwiches and the sound of lovesick crows
on the electrical lines each May. The world is a glorious
place, and filled with so many unexpected moments that I'd
get lumps in my throat, as though I were watching a bride
walk down the aisle – moments as eternal and full of love as
the lifting of veils, the saying of vows and the moment of the
first wedded kiss.

*　　*　　*

The lunch hour bell rang and the hallways erupted into
ordered hubbub. Normally I wouldn't have gone to the
cafeteria; I was part of the Out to Lunch Bunch – six girls
from the *Youth Alive!* program. We'd go down to one of the
fast-food places at the foot of the mountain for salad bar,
fries and ice water. Our one rule was that every lunch we had
to confess a sin to the group. I always made mine up: I'd
stolen a blusher from the drugstore; I'd peeked at my

brother's porn stash – nothing too big, but nothing too small, either. In the end, it was simply easier to be with five people in a restaurant booth than three hundred in a cafeteria. I was antisocial at heart. And if people knew how dull our lunches were, they'd never have bothered to waste energy calling us stuck-up. So, I was surprised when I went into the cafeteria to meet Jason to find the Bunch hogging one of the cafeteria's prime center tables. I asked, "So what's this all about?"

Their faces seemed so – *young* to me. Unburdened. Newly born. I wondered if I'd now lost what they still had, the aura of fruit slightly too unripe to pick.

Jaimie Kirkland finally said, "My dad got smashed and took out a light post on Marine Drive last night. And Dee's Cabrio has this funny smell in it since she loaned it to her grandmother, so we thought we'd go native today."

"Everyone must be flattered." I sat down. Meaningful stares pinballed from face to face, but I feigned obliviousness. Lauren was the clique's designated spokeswoman. "Cheryl, I think we should continue our talk from earlier."

"Really?"

"Yes, really."

I was trying to decide between Jell-O and fruit cocktail from the cafeteria counter.

Dee cut in: "Cheryl, I think you need to do some confessing to us." Five sets of eyes drilled into me in judgment.

"Confess to what?" Forcing them to name the deed was fun.

"You," said Lauren, "and Jason. Fornicating."

I began giggling, and I could see their righteousness

melting away like snow on a car's hood. And that was when I heard the first gunshot.

*   *   *

Jason and I connected the moment we first met (albeit through some seat switching on my part) in tenth-grade biology class. My family had just moved into the neighborhood from across town. I knew that Jason's attraction to me would go nowhere unless I learned more about his world. He appealed to me because he was so untouched by life, but I think this attraction for someone dewy clean was unnatural for a girl as young as me. I think most girls want a guy who's seen a bit of sin, who knows just a little bit more than they do about life.

Jason appeared to be heavily into *Youth Alive!*, which added to his virginal charm. I later learned that his enthusiastic participation was an illusion, fostered by the fact that Jason's older brother, Kent, two years ahead of us, was almost head of *Alive!*'s Western Canadian division; Jason was roped in and was dragged along in Kent's dust. Kent was like Jason minus the glow. When I was around Kent, I never felt that life was full of wonder and adventure; Kent made it sound as if our postschool lives were going to be about as exciting as temping in a motor vehicles office. He was always into *planning* and preparing for the *next step*. Jason was certainly not into planning. I wonder how much of our relationship was a slap on Kent's face by his brother who was tired of being scheduled into endless group activities.

In any event, Pastor Fields's sermons on chastity could only chill the blood in Jason's loins so long. So I began attending *Youth Alive!* meetings three times a week, singing

"Kumbaya," bringing along salads and standing in prayer circles – all of this, at first, just to nab Jason Klaasen and his pink chamois skin.

And I did – nab him. We were an item within the group itself, and to the rest of the school an attractive but dull couple. And not a day went by where Jason didn't ask for something more than a kiss, but I held out. I knew he was into religion just deep enough to think losing his virginity meant crossing a line.

The thing was, I *did* discover religion during my campaign to catch Jason, and that's not something I'd expected, as there was nothing in my upbringing that predisposed me to conversion. My family paid lip service to religious convictions. They were fickle – no God being feared there. My family wasn't so much anti-God as it was pro the world. God got misplaced along the way. Are they lost? Are they damned? I don't know. I'd be mistrustful of anybody who said they were, and yet here I am, in the calm dark waiting to go off into the Next Place, and I think it's a different place from where my family's headed.

My family didn't know what to make of my conversion. It's not as if I was a problem teen who rebounded into faith – the most criminal I ever got was generic teenage girl things like prank phone calls and shoplifting.

My parents seemed happy for me in a well-at-least-she's-not-dating-the-entire-basketball-team kind of way, but when I discussed going to heaven or righteousness, they became constrained and a bit sad. My younger brother, Chris, came to a few *Alive!* meetings but chose team sports instead. Truth be told, I was glad to have religion all to myself.

Dear God,
I'm going to stop believing in you unless you can tell me what possible good could have come from the bloodshed. I can't see any meaning or evidence of divine logic.

I can discuss the killings with the detachment I have from being in this new place. The world is pulling away from me, losing its capacity to hurt.

For starters, nobody screamed. That's maybe the oddest component of the killings. All of us thought the first shots were firecrackers – part of a Halloween prank, as firecracker season starts in early October. When the popping got louder, people in the cafeteria looked to its six wide doors with the expectation of being slightly amused by some young kids doing a stunt. And then this kid from the tenth grade, Mark Something, came tottering in, his chest red and purple from what looked like really bad makeup, and there were some nervous laughs in the room. Then he fell and his head landed the wrong way on the corner of a bench, like a bag of gym equipment. We heard some guys yelling, and three grade eleven students walked into the caf wearing duck-hunting outfits – military green fatigues with camouflage patterns, covered with bulging pockets and strips of ammunition – and right away one of them shot out a bank of overhead fluorescent lights. One of the suspension cables broke and a light bank fell down onto a table of food – the not-very-popular photo club and chess club table. The second guy, in sunglasses and a beret, plucked out two grade nine boys and one girl who were standing at the vending machines. These were messy shots that left a mist of blood on the ivory-colored cinder-block walls. A group of maybe ten students tried bolting for the doors, but the gunmen – gun*boys,* really – turned and showered them with buckshot or bullets, whatever it is that guns and rifles use.

Two of them got away cleanly and I could hear their footsteps echoing down the corridor. As for the rest of us, there was no escape route, so we clambered underneath the tables, as if in some ancient nuclear drill from the 1960s.

*   *   *

In the summer between grades eleven and twelve, after my conversion and after landing Jason, I had a summer job at a concession stand at Ambleside Beach. It was a dry hot summer and the two other girls I worked with were fun – kind of skinny and nutty and they mimicked the customers quite wickedly. They also didn't go to Delbrook, so they didn't have any history with me, which was a relief, and I felt guilty feeling this relief. *Youth Alive!* was concerned that my constant exposure to semiclad skin, sun and non–*Youth Alive!* members would make me revert to the World – as if listening to screaming babies and groping for the last purple Popsicle at the bottom of the freezer bin could be a test of faith or tempt me into secular drift. Lauren and Dee and some of the others visited me a bit too often, and I don't think a night ever went by without returning to my car at shift's end and finding an *Alive!*er eager to invite me to a barbecue or a hike or a Spirit Cruise around the harbor.

By the end of that August, Jason was going mental for me. He came into the city on weekends from his job up the coast, surveying for a mining company. A sample conversation from this period might go:

"Cheryl, God would never have made it feel so right or so good unless it *was* right and good."

"Jason, could you honestly hold up your head and say to Pastor Fields or your mother or the Lord that you'd been fornicating with Cheryl Anway? Could you?"

Well, of course he couldn't. There was only one way he could land what he wanted, and that was marriage. One weekend in my bedroom, he said we could get married after graduation. I removed his hand from near my right breast and said, "God doesn't issue moral credit cards, Jason. He's not like a bank. You can't borrow now and pay later."

"My strength – Cheryl, I'm losing it."

"Then pray for more. God never sends you a temptation that you aren't strong enough to overcome."

I did want Jason but, as I've said, only on my own terms, which also happened to be God's terms. I'm not sure if I used God or He used me, but the result was the same. In the end, we are judged by our deeds, not our wishes. We're the sum of our decisions.

*   *   *

During none of my lunch-hour confessions, whether at the White Spot drive-in eating fries with the Bunch, or at an *Alive!* weekend seminar on kingdom building, did I ever once confess how much I needed Jason, in every sort of way. Even thinking of him made me drunk, and all the teenage girl stuff that came with it: bees needing flowers; wanting to dissolve like sugar into tea.

Of course, everybody else in the school was going at it like minks. Nothing was forbidden to them, so why not? It's indeed a mistake to confuse children with angels. And while the ever-present aura of casual sex saturated the school like locker aroma, I didn't surrender to my own instincts, though I really did have to wonder why God makes teenagers so desperate. Why could we see Archie and Betty and Veronica on dates at the malt shop, but never screwing around in Archie's dad's basement covered in oil stains, spit and semen? Double standard. You can't do one without implying the other. Preachy me.

Dear Lord,
Protect our children, while they . . . Lord keep them as
. . . Sorry. I can't pray right now.

Dear God,
What's hardest here is that I simply can't believe this is happening. Why do You make certain kinds of events feel real, but not others? Do You have a name for this? And could You please make all of this *feel real*?

As I was saying, silence.

In the first few moments of the attack, I remember briefly seeing a patch of sky out the window and I remembered how crisp and clean the day was.

Then one of the boys shot his gun in that direction and stemmed the exodus. I know nothing about guns. Whatever they were, they were powerful, and when they cocked them, it sounded industrial, like a machine stamping something flat.

Under the tables we all dove – *thumpa-thumpa-thump*.

Don't shoot at me – I'm not making any noise! Look! Look at How! Quiet! I'm! Being!

Shoot someone else over there! Shoot me? No! Way!

I could have stood up, shouted and caused a diversion and

saved a hundred people, or organized the lifting of our table to create a shield to ram into the gunmen. But I sat there like a meek little sheep and it's the only thing I've ever done that disgusts me. Silence was my sin. I sinned as I cowered and watched three pairs of ocher-colored work boots tromp about the room, toying with us as though we were bacteria under a magnifying lens.

I recognized all of the boys – working on the yearbook is good for that kind of thing. There was Mitchell Van Waters. I remembered seeing him down at the smoke hole by the parking lot with his fellow eleventh-grade gunmen, Jeremy Kyriakis and Duncan Boyle.

I watched Mitchell, Jeremy and Duncan walk from table to table. Take away the combat fatigues and they looked like the kid who mows your lawn or shoots hoops in the driveway next door. There was nothing physically interesting about them except that Mitchell was pretty skinny and Duncan had a small port-wine birthmark inside his hairline – I knew about this only because we'd been looking at photos as part of paste-up and layout during class.

As the three walked from table to table, they talked among themselves – most of what they said I couldn't make out. Some tables they shot at; some they didn't. As the boys came nearer to us, Lauren pretended to be dead, eyes open, body limp, and I wanted to smack her, but I was just mad at myself, perhaps more than anything for being afraid. It had been drilled into us that to feel fear is to not fully trust God. Whoever made that one up has never been beneath a cafeteria table with a tiny thread of someone else's blood trickling onto their leg.

* * *

One contradiction of the human heart is this: God refuses to see any one person as unique in his or her relationship to Him, and yet we humans see each other as bottomless wells of creativity and uniqueness. *I write songs about horses; you make owl-shaped wall hangings; he combs his hair like some guy on TV; she knows the capital city of every country on earth.* Inasmuch as uniqueness is an arrogant human assumption, Jason was unique, and because of this, he was lovable. To me. First off, he was terrific with voices – ones he made up and ones he mimicked. As with the girls from my summer job, I was a sucker for anyone who could imitate others. Jason with even one beer in him was better than cable TV. He used his voices the way ventriloquists use their dummies – to say things he was too shy to say himself. Whenever a situation was boring and there was no escaping it – dinner with my family, or party games organized by Pastor Fields's wife that incorporated name tags and blindfolds – Jason went into his cat character, Mr. No, an otherwise ordinary cat who had a Nielsen TV ratings monitor box attached to his small black-and-white TV. Mr. No hated everything and he showed his displeasure by making a tiny, almost sub-audible squeaking *nee-yow* sound. I guess you had to be there. But Mr. No made more than a few painful hours a treat.

Jason could also wiggle his ears, and his arms were double-jointed – some of his contortions were utterly harrowing, and I'd scream for him to stop. He also bought me seventeen roses for my seventeenth birthday, and how many boys do you know who'd do *that*?

I was surprised when Jason did propose – in his dad's Buick on a rainy August afternoon in the White Spot parking lot over a cheeseburger and an orange float. I was surprised first because he *did it,* then second because he'd concocted a secret plan that was so wild that only the deadest of souls could refuse. Basically, using money he'd stockpiled from his summer job, we were going to fly to Las Vegas. There in the car, he produced fake IDs, a bottle of Champale and the thinnest of gold rings, barely strong enough to retain its shape. He said, "A ring is a halo for your finger. From now on, we no longer cast two shadows, we cast one."

"Fake IDs?" I asked.

"I don't know the legal age there. They're for backup."

I looked, and they seemed to be convincing fakes, with our real names and everything, with just the birth dates changed. And as it turned out, the legal age was eighteen, so we did need the fakes.

Jason asked me if I wanted to elope: "No big churchy wedding or anything?"

"Jason, marriage is marriage, and if it were as simple as pushing a button on the dash of this car, I'd do it right now."

What I didn't go on about was the sexiness of it all. Sex – *finally* – plus freedom from guilt or retribution. My only concern was that Jason would develop chilly feet and blab to his buddies or Pastor Fields. I told him that blabbing would be a deal wrecker, and I made him vow, under threat-of-hell conditions, that this would be our secret. I'd also recently been reading a book of religious inspiration geared mainly to men, and I'd dog-eared the chapter that told its readers, essentially, to trust nobody. Friends are always betrayers in the end – everybody has the one person to whom they spill everything, and that special person isn't always the obvious person you'd think. People are leaky. What kind of paranoid creep would write something like that? Well, whoever it was, it helped further my cause.

The important thing is that we were to marry in the final week of August in Las Vegas. I greased the skids at home and told my folks I was attending a hymn retreat up the coast; I told Lauren and the *Alive!* crew I was driving to Seattle with my family. Jason did the same thing. It was set.

Dear God,
I'm trying to take my mind off the slayings, but I don't know if that's possible. I'll forget about them for maybe a minute and then I'll remember again. I tried finding solace looking at the squirrels in the front yard, already gathering food for the winter – and then I got to thinking about how short their lives are – so short that their dreams can only possibly be a full mirroring of their waking lives. So I guess for a squirrel, being awake and being asleep are the same thing. Maybe when you die young it's like that, too. A baby's dream would only be the same as being awake – teenagers, too, to some extent. As I've said, I'm grasping here for some solace.

Lord,
I *know* I don't have a fish sticker, or whatever it is I'm supposed to have on my car bumper, like all those stuck-up kids who think they're holier than Thou, but I also don't think they have some sort of express lane to speak to You, so I imagine You're hearing this okay. I guess my question to You is whether or not You get to

torture those evil bastards who did the killings, or if it's purely the devil's job and You subcontract it out. Is there any way I can help torture them from down here on earth? Just give me a sign and I'm in.

What I now find odd is how Jason and I both assumed our marriage had to be a secret. It wasn't from shame, and it wasn't from fear, because eighteen is eighteen (well, almost) and the law's the law, so in the eyes of the taxman and the Lord, we could go at it like rabbits all day as long as we paid our taxes and made a few babies along the way. Sometimes life, when laid out plainly like this, can seem so simple.

What appealed to me was that this marriage was something the two of us could have entirely to ourselves, like being the only two guests in a luxury hotel. I knew that if we got engaged and waited until after high school to marry, our marriage would become something else – ours, yes, but not *quite* ours, either. There would be presents and sex lectures and unwanted intrusions. Who needs all that? And in any event, I had no pictures in my head of life after high school. My girlfriends all wanted to go to Hawaii or California and drive sports cars and, if I correctly read between the lines on the yearbook questionnaires they submitted, have serial monogamous relations with *Youth Alive!* guys that didn't necessarily end in marriage. The best I could see for myself was a house, a kid or two, some chicken noodle soup at three in the afternoon while standing at the kitchen sink watching clouds unfurl coastward from Vancouver Island.

I was sure that whatever Jason did for a living would amply fulfill us both – an unpopular sentiment among girls my age. Jason once halfheartedly inquired as to my career ambitions, and when he was certain I had none, he was relieved. His family – churchier than Thou – looked down on girls who worked. If I was ever going to get a job, it would only be to annoy *them,* his parents – his dad, mostly. He was a mean, dried-out fart who defied charity, and who used religion as a foil to justify his undesirable character traits. His cheapness became *thrift;* his lack of curiosity about the world and his contempt for new ideas were called *being traditional.*

Jason's mother was, well, there's no way around it, a bit drunk the few times I met her. I don't think she liked the way her life had played out. Who am I to judge? How the two of them procreated a sweetie-pie like Jason remains one of God's true mysteries.

*   *   *

If nothing else, relating the step-by-step course of events in the cafeteria allows me to comprehend how distanced from the world I'm feeling now – how quickly the world is pulling away. And for this reason I'll continue.

After the first dozen shots, the fire alarm went off. Mitchell Van Waters walked to the main cafeteria doors, said, "Goddammit," and fired into the hall, blasting out the bell ringing there. Jeremy Kyriakis took out the cafeteria's fire bell in three shots, after which a hail of drywall particles pinged and rattled throughout the otherwise silent room. Beneath the tables we could still hear fire bells ringing from deep within the school's bowels, bells that would ring past sunset since the RCMP would hold off disabling the central OFF switch for fear of tripping homemade bombs placed throughout the school – bombs made of benzene and powdered swimming-pool cleaner. Wait – how did I know that combo? Oh yes, Mitchell Van Waters's contribution to the science fair: "Getting the Most Bang for Your Buck." It was in last year's yearbook.

Back to the cafeteria.

Back to me and three hundred other students under the tables, either dead or playing dead, scrunching themselves into tiny balls. Back to six work boots clomping on the polished putty-colored linoleum, and the sounds of ambulances and RCMP cruisers whooping schoolward, a little too little, a little too late.

I began doing a numbers game in my head. Three hundred people divided among three gunmen makes a hundred victims per gunman. If they were going to kill us all, it would take a bit of time, so I figured my chances of making it were better than I'd first supposed. But geographically we were in a bad spot: the center of the room, the visual and architectural core of the place, as well as the nexus of any high school's social ambition and peer envy. Were people envious of Alivers!? We were basically invisible in the school. A few students might have thought we were small-minded and clique-ish, and to be honest, *Youth Alive!* members *were*. But I wasn't. In general, as I walked about the school I affected a calm, composed smile. I did this not because I wanted to be everyone's friend – or to avoid making enemies – but simply because it was easier and I didn't need to interact. A bland smile is like a green light at an intersection – it feels good when you get one, but you forget it the moment you're past it.

Dear Lord,
If You organized a massacre just to make people have doubts, then maybe You ought to consider other ways

of doing things. A high school massacre? Kids with pimento loaf sandwiches and cans of Orange Crush? I don't think You would orchestrate something like this. A massacre in a high school cafeteria can only indicate Your absence – that for some reason, in some manner, You chose to absent Yourself from the room. Forsake it, actually.

Cheryl – the pretty girl who was the last one to be shot. She wrote that in her binder, didn't she? "God is nowhere." Maybe she was right.

Dear God,

I'm out of prayers, so that just leaves talking. It's hard for me to believe other people are feeling as intensely as I do, and as bad as I do. But then, if we're all as messed up as I am, that scares me into thinking that the world's all going to go to pieces, and what sort of world would *that* be? A zoo.

I keep to myself mostly. I can't sleep or eat. TV stinks. School's closed for a while yet. I smoked pot and it wasn't a good idea. I walk around in a daze and it's like the opposite of drugs, because drugs are supposed to make you feel good, but this only makes me feel bad.

I was walking down at the mall, and suddenly I started hitting myself in the head because I thought I could bash away the feelings. And the thing is, everybody in the mall looked as if they knew what I was doing, and no one flipped out.

Anyway, this is where I stand now. I'm not sure this was a prayer. I don't know what it was.

I've not been too specific about my life and my particulars, but by now you must have gleaned a few things about who I was – Cheryl Anway. The papers are blanketing the world with my most recent yearbook photo, and if you've seen it then you'll know I was a cliché girl next door: darkish blond hair cut in a way that'll probably look stupid to future students, with a thin face and, on the day the photos were taken, no pimples – how often did *that* ever happen? In the photo I look old for seventeen. I'm smiling the smile I used when passing people in the halls without having to speak to them.

The description accompanying my photo is along the lines of "Cheryl was a good student, friendly and popular" – and that's about it. What a waste of seventeen years. Or is that just my selfish heart applying standards of the world to a soul that's eternal? It is. But by seventeen, nobody ever accomplishes anything, do they? Joan of Arc? Anne Frank? And maybe some musicians and actresses. I'd really like to ask God why it is that we don't accomplish anything until we're at least twenty. Why the wait? I think we should be born ten years old, and then after a year turn twenty – just get it over with, like dogs do. We ought to be born running.

Chris and I had a dog, a spaniel named Sterling. We adored Sterling, but Sterling adored gum. We'd go for walks and all he'd do was sniff out sidewalk discards. It was cute and funny, but when I was in grade nine he ate a piece of something that wasn't gum, and two hours later he was gone. We buried him in the backyard beneath the witch hazel shrub, and I put a cross on his grave, a cross my mother removed after my conversion. I found it in the garden shed between the 5–20–20 and a stack of empty black plastic nursery pots, and I was too chicken to ask her why.

I don't worry too much about Sterling, as he's in heaven. Animals never left God – only people did. Lucky animals.

My father works in the mortgage division of Canada Trust, and my mother is a technician in a medical lab. They love their jobs. Chris is a generic little brother, yet not as snotty or pesky as my friends' little brothers.

At Christmas everyone in our family exchanged bad sweaters and we all wore them as a kind of in-joke. So we were one of those bad-sweater families you see at the mall.

We got along with each other – or we did until recently. It's like we decided to be superficially happy with each other, which is fine, and that we wouldn't share intimacies with each other. I don't know. I think that lack of sharing weakened us.

Dear Lord,
I pray for the souls of the three killers, but I don't know if that is right or wrong.

It always seemed to me that people who'd discovered religion had both lost and gained something. Outwardly, they'd gained calmness, confidence and a look of purpose, but what they'd lost was a certain willingness to connect with unconverted souls. Looking a convert in the eyes was like trying to make eye contact with a horse. They'd be alive and breathing, but they wouldn't be a hundred percent *there* anymore. They'd left the day-to-day world and joined the realm of eternal time. Pastor Fields or Dee or Lauren would have pounced on me if I'd ever spoken those words aloud. Dee would have said something like "Cheryl, you've just covered your halo with soot. Repent. Now."

There can be an archness, a meanness in the lives of the saved, an intolerance that can color their view of the weak and of the lost. It can make them hard when they ought to be listening, judgmental when they ought to be contrite.

Jason's father, Reg, always said, "Love what God loves and hate what God hates," but more often than not I had the impression that he really meant "Love what Reg loves and hate what Reg hates." I don't think he imparted this philosophy to Jason. Jason was too gentle, too forgiving, to adopt Reg's self-serving credo. As my mother always told me, "Cheryl, trust me, you spend a much larger part of your life being old, not young. Rules change along the way. The first things to go are those things you thought were eternal."

*   *   *

Getting married in Nevada in 1988 was simple. At noon on the final Friday before school started, Jason and I cabbed out to the airport and scanned the list of outgoing flights. There was one to Las Vegas in ninety minutes, so we bought tickets – cash – walked through U.S. Immigration preclearance, went to the gate and were on our way. They didn't even bother to check our ID. We each had only a gym bag for carry-on and we felt like bandits. It was my first time flying, and everything was new and charged with mystery . . . the laminated safety cards, the takeoff, which made my stomach cartwheel, the food, which was bad just like they always joke about on TV, and the cigarette smoke; something about Las Vegas attracts the smokers. But it was all like perfume to me, and I tried pretending that every moment of my life could be as full of newness as that flight. What a life that would be.

The two of us had dressed conservatively – shirt and tie for Jason, and me in a schoolmarm dress; our outfits must have made us look all of fifteen. The flight attendant asked us why we were going to Las Vegas and we told her. Ten minutes later there was a captain's announcement telling everybody on the plane our news and our seat numbers. The other passengers clapped and I blushed like I had a fever, but suddenly it was as if we were blood kin with all these strangers. At the terminal, the men all slapped Jason's back and har-har'ed, and this one woman whispered to me, "Honey, I don't care what else you do, but the moment he hints that he wants it, you give it to him. Doesn't matter if you're fixing a diaper or cleaning out the gutters. You give it, pronto. Else you'll lose him."

It was over a hundred degrees outside, my first exposure to genuine heat, Jason's too. My lungs had never felt so pure. In the taxi to Caesars Palace I looked out at the desert – real *desert* – and tried to imagine every parable I'd ever heard taking place in that exotic lifeless nothingness. I couldn't have stood five minutes out there in that oven, and I wondered how the Bible ever managed to happen. They must have had different weather back then – or trees – or rivers and shade. Good Lord, the desert is harsh. I asked the taxi driver to stop for a second beside a vacant lot between the airport and the Strip. There were some rental units on the other side of a cinder-block fence, some litter and a shedded snakeskin. I got out and it felt as if I were floating over the sharp rocks and angry little plants. Instead of feeling brand new, Las Vegas felt thousands of years old. Jason got out and we both knelt and prayed. Time passed; I felt dizzy and the cabbie honked the horn. We drove to Caesars Palace.

*   *   *

I knew we were goners when Dee knocked over an apple juice can. *Clank*. The three boys had been across the room shouting pointless fragments of pointless manifestos or whatever moronic ideas they had, but then, yes, the *clank*. It was so primal to watch their heads swivel toward us, and their eyes focusing – zeroing in like crocodiles in TV documentaries. Dee squeaked.

I heard Duncan Boyle say, "Oh, if it isn't the Out to Lunch Bunch slumming with us, the damned, here in purgatory, School District 44." Listening to the inflections of his voice, for just a second I thought to myself that he could sing if he wanted to. I could always tell that about people – if they could sing or not.

Just then, for whatever reason, the overhead sprinklers spritzed on. The boys were distracted and looked up at the ceiling. The water rained down onto the tables, onto the milk cartons and half-empty paper bags; it sounded like rain on a roof. Then it began trickling off the laminated tabletops and dripping onto my jeans and forearms. It was cold and I shivered and Lauren was shivering, too. I put my arm around her and held her to me, her teeth chattering like maracas. Then there were more shots – at us, I assumed, but Mitchell Van Waters blew out some of the sprinkler nozzles, shattering a large pipe, and the water came down on us in buckets.

There was a noise from outside the building and Martin Boyle shouted, "Windows!" He and Mitchell blasted out four large panes opposite us. Then Duncan asked, "Was that a cop I saw out there?"

"What do you think?" Mitchell was mad as hornets. "Rearm!"

The guns made more metallic noises and Mitchell blew out the remaining windows. The school was now like a jewel case encrusted with snipers and cops. Their time with their victims was drawing to an end.

Lord,
I know that faith is not the natural condition of the human heart, but why do You make it so hard to have faith? Were we so far gone here in boring North Van that we needed a shock treatment? There are thousands of suburbs as average as us. Why us then? And why now? You raise the cost of faith and You dilute its plausibility. Is that smart?

Dear God,
I keep on imagining what those kids under the tables must have been feeling and it only makes me angrier and crazier at You. It just does.

Dear God,
I'm prayed out, and yet here I am, still knocking on Your door, but I think this could be the last time.

Dear Lord,
This is the first time I've ever prayed because I didn't grow up with this stuff, but here I am, praying away, so maybe there's something to it. Maybe I'm wasting my time. You tell me. Send me a sign. You must get a lot of that. Proof proof proof. Because to my mind, the

school massacre could mean that You *don't* exist just as much – if not *more* than – it could mean that You do. If I was trying to recruit followers, a school massacre isn't the way I'd go about doing it. But then it got me here right now, praying, didn't it?

Just so you know, I'm having my first drink here as I pray my first prayer – apricot liqueur, I skimmed off the top inch of my dad's bottle. It tastes like penicillin and I like it.

I've never told anyone about the moment of my conversion in eleventh grade. I was by myself, out in the backyard in fall, sitting between two huckleberry shrubs that had survived the mountainside's suburban development. I closed my eyes and faced the sun and that was that – *ping!* – the sensation of warmth on my eyelids and the smell of dry cedar and fir branches in my nose. I never expected angels and trumpets, nor did any appear. The moment made me feel special, and yet, of course, nothing makes a person less special than conversion – it . . . *universalizes* you.

But then how special can any person really be? I mean, you have a name and some ancestors. You have medical, educational and work histories, as well as immediate living family and friends. And after that there's not much more. At least in my case. At the time of my death, my life's résumé consisted of school, sports, a few summer jobs and my *Youth Alive!* involvement. My death was the only remarkable aspect of my life. I'm rummaging through my memories trying to find even a few things to distinguish me from all others. And yet . . . and yet I was *me* – nobody saw the world as I did, nor did they feel the things I felt. I was Cheryl Anway: that has to count for something.

And I did have questions and uneasy moments after my conversion. I wondered why it is that going to heaven is the only goal of religion, because it's such a selfish thing. The Out to Lunch Bunch talked about going to heaven in the same breath as they discussed hair color. Leading a holy life inside a burgundy-colored VW Cabrio seems like a spiritual contradiction. Jason once joked that if you read Revelations closely, you could see where it says that Dee Carswell counting the calories in a packet of Italian dressing is a sign of imminent apocalypse. And yet we all possessed the capacity for slipping at any moment into great sin and eternal darkness. I suppose it's what made me a bit withdrawn from the world – maybe I just didn't trust anybody fully, knowing how close we all were to the edge. That's not true: I trusted Jason.

Whenever I felt doubts I overcompensated by trying to witness to whoever was nearby, usually my family. And when they even remotely sensed religion coming up, they either nodded politely or they bolted. I can't imagine what they said about me when I wasn't there. In any event, I think in the end it's maybe best to keep your doubts private. Saying them aloud cheapens them – makes them a bunch of words just like everybody else's bunch of words.

*   *   *

I don't think I fully understood sleaze until Jason and I entered the chilled lobby of Caesars Palace on that day of burning winds and X-ray sunlight. It stank of American cigarettes, smoky blue and tarlike, and of liquor. A woman dressed up like a centurion with balloon boobs and stage makeup asked us for our drink order. She reminded me of a novelty cocktail shaker. The thing is, we said yes, and Jason ordered two gin fizzes – where did *that* come from? They arrived within moments and there we stood, dumb as planks, while the most desperate sort of gamblers – I mean, this was August in the middle of the desert – slunk past us, serenaded by the endless rattling and dinging of the slot machines. I don't think I'd ever seen so many souls teetering so precariously on the brink of colossal sin. Hypocritical me. We're all equally on the brink of all sins.

We went up to our room: shabby and yellowing. I couldn't figure out why such a splashy place would have such dumpy rooms, but Jason said it was to drive people down into the casinos.

Once the door was closed, it was a bit awkward. Until then, it had all felt like a field trip. We sat on the edge of the bed and Jason asked if I still wanted to get married, and I said yes – I'd caught a sliver of his naked behind through the bathroom door's hinge crack as he changed into his other pair of pants.

As we sat there, we realized our clothes, even in the air-conditioned room, were far too hot for the climate. Jason shed his tie, and I replaced my all-concealing "skin is sin" dress with a jacket and skirt, the only other garments I'd brought – something like you'd wear to work on a Wednesday morning.

Sooner than I'd have liked we were out the door, appearing to the world as if we were headed to a $2.99 all-you-can-eat shrimp buffet or to lose ourselves for a few hours in front of the dime slots with the pensioners. We were alone in the elevator and kissed briefly, and then we staggered through the lobby bombarded again by a wash of noise and sleaze.

Outside it was nearing sunset. An ashtray on wheels picked us up. The cabbie was a fat guy with an East Coast accent and exactly one hair on his forehead, just like Charlie Brown. He slapped the steering wheel when we asked him to take us to a chapel. He told us his name, Evan, and we asked him if he'd be our witness. He said sure, he'd stand up for us, and for the first time that day I felt not just as if I was getting married, but also like a *bride*.

The chapels were itty-bitty things, and we tried to find one in which celebrities had never been married, as if a celebrity aura could somehow crush the holy dimension of a Las Vegas wedding. I don't know what we were thinking. Evan ended up choosing a chapel for us, mostly because it included a snack platter and sparkling wine in the price of the service.

There was paperwork; our fake IDs aroused no suspicion. Out the little stained-glass window up front the sun was like a juicy tangerine on the horizon. Quickly, a dramatically tanned man in white rayon, who might just as easily have been offering us a deal on a condominium time-share, declared us legally wed.

Nearing the front door, Jason said, "Well, it's not quite two hundred and fifty of our nearest and dearest, is it?"

I was so giddy: "A civil wedding. What would your *dad* say?"

We went outside, leaving Evan to his snack platter – out into the hot air scented by exhaust fumes, snapdragons and litter, just the two of us, dwarfed by the casinos and dreaming of the future, of the lights, both natural and false, appearing in the sky, and of sex.

*　　　*　　　*

I hoped that both the shooting of the windows and the flooding sprinklers would distract the three boys, but this didn't happen. Instead, they began to fight among themselves. Mitchell was furious with Jeremy for wasting ammunition that could be more effectively used "killing those stuck-up pigs who feed on taunting anybody who doesn't have a numbered sweater." To this end, Mitchell fired across the room, into a huddled mass of younger students – the junior jocks, I think, but I can't be very sure, because the tabletops and chairs blocked my view. I also didn't know whether the gunshots scattered or formed a concentrated beam, but I clearly remember blood from the huddle mixing with the streams of sprinkler water that trickled along the linoleum's slight slant, down to behind the bank of vending machines. The machines made a quick electrical fizz noise and went dead. From the huddle came a few screams, some moans and then silence. Mitchell shouted, "We know that most of you aren't dead or even wounded, so don't think we're stupid. Duncan, should we go over and see who's fibbing and who isn't?"

"I don't know – I could get a bit more pumped about all of this if saggy-assed Jeremy would start pulling his weight."

The two turned to Jeremy, the least talkative of the three. Mitchell said, "What's the matter – deciding to convert into a jock all of a sudden? Gee, won't that make the Out to Lunch Bunch hot for you. A killer with a heart of gold."

Jeremy said, "Mitchell, shut up. Like we haven't noticed that all *your* shots are missing their mark? The only reason you shot out the windows was because it's impossible to miss them."

Mitchell got angrier. "You know what? I think *you're* jamming out, and you're jamming out a little bit too late into the game, I think."

"What if I *was* to jam out?"

Mitchell said, "Watch this," and fired across the room, killing a boy named Clay, whose locker was four down from mine. "There, see? Killing is fun. Jam out now, and you're next."

"I quit."

"No, Jeremy, it's too late for that. Duncan, what would you guess Jeremy's tally up to this moment has been?"

Duncan calculated. "Four definite hits and five maybes."

Mitchell turned to Jeremy: "Ha! And you expect mercy from the world?"

"I quit."

Mitchell said, "What do we have here – a Hitler-in-the-bunker scenario?"

"Call it what you will." Jeremy dropped his weapons.

Mitchell said, "Execution time."

*   *   *

Being married was wild. It was worth all the delays and pleas and postponement of pleasure, and you know, this isn't some guidance-class hygiene film speaking to you – it's me. I was *me*. We were *us*. It was all real, and wild, and it is my most cherished memory of having been alive – a night of abandon on the sixteenth floor of Caesars Palace.

I doubt we said even three words to each other all night; Jason's dewy antler-soft skin made words feel stupid. By six in the morning we were in a cab headed back to the airport. On the flight north, we didn't speak much, either. And I *felt* married. I loved the sensation, and it's why I remained silent

– trying to pinpoint the exact nature of this new buzz: sex, certainly, but more than that, too.

Of course, the Out to Lunch Bunch and all of the *Alive!* crew could tell right away that something was up. We simply didn't care as much for the group as before, and it showed. The corny little lunchtime confessions over french fries were so dull as to be unlistenable; Pastor Fields's team sports metaphors and chastity pleas seemed equally juvenile to Jason. We knew what we had, and we knew what we wanted, and we knew that we wanted *more*. Then there was the issue of how we were going to go about telling our families. Jason imagined a formal dinner at a good restaurant during which to break the news – between the main course and the dessert – but I said I didn't want our marriage to be treated like a chorus girl jumping out of a cake. I'm not clear if Jason's desire for a formal dinner was his concept of maturity, or if he wanted to shock a crowd like an evil criminal mastermind. He did have his exhibitionist streak: I mean, in Las Vegas he'd refused to close the curtains and he was always trying to sneak me into the change room at the Bootlegger jeans store. No go.

So yes, we'd had a fight on the phone about this matter the night before my pregnancy test. Jason was angry with me for dragging my heels about announcing the marriage, and I was angry with him for wanting to be a – I don't know – a *show-off*.

And that's as far as I got in my life, my baby as well. I don't think I've concealed anything here, and there's not much left to explain. God owns everything. I was not replaceable, but nor was I indispensable. It was my time.

Dear God,

I am so full of hate that I'm scaring myself. Is there a word to describe wanting to kill people who are already dead? Because that's what's in my heart. I remember last year being in the backyard with my father. We lifted up this sheet of plywood that had been lying on the grass all winter. Underneath were thousands of worms, millipedes, beetles and a snake, all either eating or being eaten, and that is my heart, and the hate and the insects grow and grow blacker by the hour. I want to kill the killers, and I just can't believe that this would be a sin.

Lord,

My son described the blood and water pooling on the cafeteria floor, coating it like Varathane. He told me about the track marks left in blood by running shoes, by bare feet and by bodies either dragging themselves or being dragged away by friends. There's something else he's not telling me – a father knows that – but what could be more horrible than – Oh God, this is not a prayer.

I can't help but wonder if the other girls thought I used God as an excuse to hook up with Jason, or that I confused one with the other. Maybe I wasn't truly in love with Jason; maybe it was just an infatuation, or maybe it was only some sort of animal need like any teenager feels.

Listen to me, practical Cheryl, covering my bases, even after death. But I know that when I was alive I did face these questions: I loved Jason, but what I felt for God was different altogether. I kept them separate.

*   *   *

As Mitchell was aiming at me, there were sirens outside, helicopters, alarm bells throughout the school and water splashing down from the shattered pipe. As well, Duncan was egging Mitchell on to kill Jeremy, too, and my hopes had flip-flopped – now I thought I might survive. Then Jeremy said, "Go ahead, Mitchell, shoot me – like I care."

Mitchell seemed to be short-circuiting. He hadn't anticipated this scenario. He turned a bit to his left, looked down at me and the Bunch, then took his rifle and shot me on my left side. He really wasn't a good shot, because he was five paces away, and I should have been dead instantly. And quite honestly, it didn't hurt, the shooting, and I didn't die immediately, either. Lauren, bless her, lunged away from me, leaving me there on the floor on top of my binder, which the water had sloshed off the tabletop. At my new angle, I could see much better what was transpiring. Mitchell said, "Well, Jeremy, you stud, that's one less girl for you to impress," and Jeremy said, "Dear God, I repent for my sins. Forgive me for all I have done."

In unison, Mitchell and Duncan shrieked, "What?" and turned to Jeremy, blasted him enough to kill him a dozen times over. Then I heard Jason's voice from the cafeteria doors – something along the lines of *"Put those guns down now."*

Mitchell said, "You have *got* to be kidding."

"I'm not kidding."

Mitchell shot at Jason and missed, and then I saw something that looked like a lump of gray art-class clay fly through the air and crack Mitchell on the side of his head, so fiercely that I could see his skull implode.

At this point, the boys in the camera club lifted up their table and used it as a shield as they charged against the sole surviving gunman, Duncan Boyle. It was covered with paper bags and some cookies that had been glued in place by blood. They charged into Duncan, pressing him against a blank spot of cinder-block wall. I saw the rifle fall to the ground, and then I saw the boys from the camera club laying the table flat on the ground on top of Duncan and begin jumping up and down on it like a grape press. They were making hooting noises, and people from the other tables came and joined in and the table became a killing game as all of these children, boys and girls, who fifteen minutes earlier had been peacefully eating peanut butter sandwiches and oranges, became savages, killing without pause. Duncan's blood dribbled out from under the table.

Lauren called out, and Jason came over and lifted the table off me like a hurricane lifting off a roof. I know he said something to me, but my hearing was gone. He tried holding me up, but my neck was limp, and all I could see was across the room, children crushing other children. And that was that.

*   *   *

To acknowledge God is to fully accept the sorrow of the human condition. And I believe I accepted God, and I fully accepted this sorrow, even though until the events in the cafeteria, there hadn't been too much of it in my life. I may have looked like just another stupid teenage girl, but it was all in there – God, and sorrow and its acceptance.

And now I'm neither dead nor alive, neither awake nor

41

asleep, and soon I'm headed off to the Next Place, but my Jason will continue amid the living.

Oh, Jason. In his heart, he knows I'll at least be trying to watch him from beyond, whatever beyond may be. And in his heart, I think, he's now learned what I came to believe, which is, as I've said all along, that the sun may burn brightly, and the faces of children may be plump and achingly sweet, but in the air we breathe, in the water we drink and in the food we share, there will always be darkness in this world.

Part Two

1999: Jason

You won't see me in any of the photographs after the massacre – you know the ones I mean: the wire service shots of the funerals, students felt-penning teenage poetry on Cheryl's casket; teenage prayer groups in sweats and scrunchies huddled on the school's slippery gym floor; 6:30 A.M. prayer breakfasts in the highway off-ramp chain restaurants, with all the men wearing ties while dreaming of hash browns. I'm in none of them, and if you *had* seen me, I sure wouldn't have been praying.

I want to say that right from the start.

Just one hour ago, I was a good little citizen in a Toronto-Dominion bank branch over in North Van, standing in line, and none of this was even on my mind. I was there to deposit a check from my potbellied contractor boss, Les, and I was wondering if I should blow off the afternoon's work. My hand reached down into my pocket, and instead of a check, my sunburnt fingers removed the invitation to my brother's memorial service. I felt as if I'd just opened all the windows of a hot muggy car.

I folded it away and wrote down today's date on the

deposit slip. I checked the wall calendar – August 19, 1999 – and *What the heck*, I wrote a whole row of zeroes before the year, so that the date read: August 19, 00000001999. Even if you hated math, which I certainly do, you'd know that this is still mathematically the same thing as 1999.

When I gave the slip and the check to the teller, Dean, his eyes widened, and he looked up at me as if I'd handed him a holdup note. "Sir," he said, "this isn't a proper date."

I said, "Yes, it is. What makes you think it isn't?"

"The extra zeroes."

Dean was wearing a deep blue shirt, which annoyed me. "What is your point?" I asked.

"Sir, the year is nineteen ninety-nine, *not* zero zero zero zero zero zero zero one nine nine nine."

"It's the same thing."

"No, it's not."

"I'd like to speak with the branch manager."

Dean called over Casey, a woman who was maybe about my age, and who had the pursed hardness of someone who spends her days delivering bad news to people and knows she'll be doing it until her hips shatter. Casey and Dean had a hushed talk, and then she spoke to me. "Mr. Klaasen, may I ask you why you've written this on your slip?"

I stood my ground: "Putting more zeroes in front of '1999' doesn't make the year any different."

"Technically, no."

"Look, I hated math as much as you probably did – "

"I didn't hate math, Mr. Klaasen."

Casey was on the spot, but then so was I. It's not as if I'd walked into the bank planning all those extra zeroes. They just happened, and now I had to defend them. "Okay. But maybe what the zeroes *do* point out is that in a billion years – and there *will* be a billion years – we'll all be dust. Not even dust: we'll be *molecules*."

Silence.

I said, "Just think, there are still a few billion years of time out there, just waiting to happen. Billions of years, and we're not going to be here to see them."

Silence.

Casey said, "Mr. Klaasen, if this is some sort of joke, I can try to understand its abstract humor, but I don't think this slip meets the requirements of a legal banking document."

Silence.

I said, "But doesn't it make you think? Or *want* to think?"

"About what?"

"About what happens to us after we die."

This was my real mistake. Dean telegraphed Casey a savvy little glance, and in a flash I knew that they knew about me, about Cheryl, about 1988 and about my reputation as a borderline nutcase – *He never really got over it, you know.* I'm used to this. I was furious but kept my cool. I said, "I think I'd like to close my account – convert to cash, if I could."

The request was treated with the casualness I might have received if I'd asked them to change a twenty. "Of course. Dean, could you help Mr. Klaasen close out his account?"

I asked, "That's it? 'Dean, could you help Mr. Klaasen close out his account?' No debate? No questions?"

Casey looked at me. "Mr. Klaasen, I have two daughters and I can barely think past next month's mortgage, let alone the year two billion one thousand nine hundred ninety-nine. My hunch is that you'd be happier elsewhere. I'm not trying to get rid of you, but I think you know where I'm coming from."

She wasn't wearing a wedding band. "Can I take you out to lunch?" I asked.

"*What?*"

"Dinner, then."

"No!" The snaking line was eavesdropping big time. "Dean, there should be no complications in closing Mr. Klaasen's account." She looked at me. "Mr. Klaasen, I have to go."

My anger became gray emotional fuzz, and I just wanted to leave. Inside of five minutes, Dean had severed my connection to his bank, and I stood on the curb smoking a hand-rolled cigarette, my shirt untucked and $5,210.00 stuffed into the pockets of my green dungarees. I decided to leave the serene, heavily bylawed streets of North Vancouver and drive to West Vancouver, down near the ocean. At the Seventeenth and Bellevue CIBC I opened a checking account, and when I looked behind the tellers I saw an open vault. I asked if it was possible to rent a safety deposit box, which took all of three minutes to do. That box is where I'm going to place all of this, once it's finished. And here's the deal: if I get walloped by a bus next year, this letter is going to be placed in storage until May 30, 2019, when you, my two nephews, turn twenty-one. If I hang around long enough, I might hand it to you in person. But for now, that's where this letter is headed.

Just so you know, I've been writing all of this in the cab of my truck, parked on Bellevue, down by Ambleside Beach, near the pier with all its bratty kids on rollerblades and the Vietnamese guys with their crab traps pursuing *E. coli*. I'm using a pen embossed with "Travelodge" and I'm writing on the back of Les's pink invoice forms. The wind is heating up – God, it feels nice on my face – and I feel, in the most SUV-commercial sense of the word, *free*.

* * *

How to start?

First off, Cheryl and I were married. No one knows that but me, and now you. It was insane, really. I was seventeen and starved for sex, but I was still stuck in my family's religious warp, so only husband/wife sex was allowed, and even then for procreation only, and even *then* only while both partners wore heavy wool tweeds so as to drain the act of pleasure. So when I suggested to Cheryl that we fly to Las Vegas and get hitched, she floored me when she said yes. It was an impulsive request I made after our math class saw an educational 16mm film about gambling. The movie was supposed to make high school students more enthusiastic about statistics. I mean, what were these filmmakers thinking?

And what was *I* thinking? Marriage? Las *Vegas*?

We flew down there one weekend and – I mean, we weren't even people then, we were so young and out of it. We were like baby chicks. No. We were like zygotes, little zygotes cabbing from the airport to Caesars Palace, and all I could think about was how hot and dry the air was. In any event, it seems like a billion years ago.

Around sunset, we got married, using our fake IDs. Our witness was a slob of a cabbie who drove us down the Strip. For the next six weeks my grades evaporated, sports became a nuisance, and my friends became ghosts. The only thing that counted was Cheryl, and because we kept the marriage secret, it was way better and more *forbidden* feeling than if we'd waited and done all the sensible stuff.

There were some problems when we got home. This churchy group Cheryl and I were in, *Youth Alive!*, crabby morality spooks who spied on us for weeks, likely with the blessing of my older brother, Kent. When I was in twelfth grade, Kent was in second year at the University of Alberta, but he was still a honcho, and I can only imagine the phone conversations he must have been having with the local *Alive!* creeps:

Were the lights on or off?

Which lights?

Did they order in pizza?

What time did they leave?

Separately or together?

As if we hadn't noticed we were being spied on. Yet in fairness, the *Alive!*ers were baby chicks, too. We all were. Seventeen is nothing. You're still in the womb.

*   *   *

There are a number of things a woman can tell about a man who is roughly twenty-nine years old, sitting in the cab of a pickup truck at 3:37 in the afternoon on a weekday, facing the Pacific, writing furiously on the back of pink invoice slips. Such a man may or may not be employed, but regardless, there is *mystery* there. If this man is with a dog, then that's good, because it means he's capable of forming relationships. But if the dog is a male dog, that's probably a bad sign, because it means the guy is likely a dog, too. A girl dog is much better, but if the guy is over thirty, any kind of dog is a bad sign regardless, because it means he's stopped trusting humans altogether. In general, if nothing else, guys my age with dogs are going to be *work*.

Then there's stubble: stubble indicates a possible drinker, *but* if he's driving a van or a pickup truck, he hasn't hit bottom yet, so watch out, honey. A guy writing something on a clipboard while facing the ocean at 3:37 P.M. may be writing poetry, or he may be writing a letter begging someone for forgiveness. But if he's writing real words, not just a job estimate or something business-y, then more likely than not this guy has something emotional going on, which could mean he has a soul.

Maybe you're generous and maybe you assume that everybody has a soul. I'm not so sure. I know that I have one, even though I'd like to reject my father's every tenet, and say I don't. But I do. It feels like a small glowing ember buried deep inside my guts.

I also believe people can be born without souls; my father believes this, too, possibly the sole issue we agree upon. I've never found a technical term for such a person – "monster" doesn't quite nail it – but I believe it to be true.

That aside, I think you can safely say that a guy in West Vancouver facing the ocean writing stuff on a clipboard in the midafternoon has troubles. If I've learned anything in twenty-nine years, it's that every human being you see in the course of a day has a problem that's sucking up at least 70 percent of his or her radar. My gift – bad choice of words – is that I can look at you, him, her, them, whoever, and tell right away what is keeping them awake at night: money; feelings of insignificance; overwhelming boredom; evil children; job troubles; or perhaps death, in one of its many costumes, perched in the wings. What surprises me about humanity is that in the end such a narrow range of plights defines our moral lives.

Whuppp . . . Joyce, my faithful white Lab, just bolted upright. What's up, girl, huh? *Up* is a Border collie with an orange tennis ball in his mouth: Brodie, Joyce's best friend. Time for an interruption – she's giving me that look.

*   *   *

An hour later:

For what it's worth, I think God is how you deal with everything that's out of your own control. It's as good a definition as any. And I have to . . .

Wait: Joyce, beside me on the bench seat, having chewed her tennis ball into fragments, is obviously wondering why we should be parked so close to a beach yet not be throwing sticks into the ocean. Joyce never runs out of energy.

Joyce, honey, hang in there. Papa's a social blank with a liver like the Hindenburg, *and he's embarrassed by how damaged he is and by how mediocre he turned out. And yes, your moist-eyed stare is a Ginsu knife slicing my heart in two like a beefsteak tomato – but I won't stop writing for a little while just yet.*

As you can see, I talk to dogs. All animals, really. They're much more direct than people. I knew that even before the massacre. Most people think I'm a near mute. Cheryl did. I wish I were a dog. I wish I were any animal other than a human being, even a bug.

Joyce, by the way, was rejected by the Seeing Eye program because she's too small. Should reincarnation exist, I'd very much like to come back as a Seeing Eye dog. No finer calling exists. Joyce joined my life nearly a year ago, at the age of four months. I met her via this crone of a Lab breeder on Bowen Island whose dream kitchen I helped install. The dream kitchen was bait to tempt her Filipina housekeeper from fleeing to the big city. Joyce was the last of the litter, the gravest, saddest pup I'd ever seen. She slept on my leather coat during the days and then spelunked into my armpits for warmth during breaks. That breeder was no dummy. After a few weeks she said, "Look, you two are in love. You *do* know that, don't you?" I hadn't thought of it that way, but once the words were spoken, it was obvious. She said, "I think you were meant for each other. Come in on the weekend and put the double-pane windows in the TV room, and she's yours." Of course I installed the windows.

*   *   *

It's a bit later again, still here in the truck, looking again at the invitation to Kent's memorial this evening.

A year ago today, I got a phone call from Barb, your mother, who had married my rock-solid brother, Kent, to much familial glee in 1995. I was driving home along the highway from a Hong Konger's home renovation at the top of the British Properties, and it was maybe six-ish, and I was wondering what bar to go to, whom to call, when the cell phone rang. Remember, this was 1998, and cell phones were a dollar-a-minute back then – hard to operate, too.

"Jason, it's Barb."

"Barb! Que pasa?"

"Jason, are you driving?"

"I am. Quitting time."

"Jason, pull over."

"Huh?"

"You heard me."

"Barb, could you maybe – "

"Jason, Jesus, just pull to the side of the road."

"Sorry I exist, Eva Braun." I pulled onto the shoulder near the Westview exit. Your mother, as you must well know by now, likes to control a situation.

"Have you pulled over?"

"Yes, Barb."

"Are you in park?"

"Barb, is micromanaging men your single biggest turn-on in life?"

"I've got bad news."

"What."

"Kent's dead."

I remember watching three swallows play in the heat rising from the asphalt. I asked, "How?"

"The police said he was gone in a flash. No pain, no warning. No fear. But he's gone."

*   *   *

Let me follow another thread. On the day of the massacre, Cheryl arrived late to school. We'd had words on the phone the night before, and when I looked out my chem class window and saw her Chevette pull into the student lot, I walked out of the classroom without asking permission. I went to her locker and we had words, intense words over how we were going to tell the world about our marriage. A few people noticed us and later said we were having a huge blowout.

We agreed to meet in the cafeteria at noon. Once this was settled, the rest of the morning was inconsequential. After the shootings, dozens of students and staff testified that I had seemed (a) preoccupied; (b) distant; and (c) as if I had something "really big" on my mind.

When the noon bell rang, I was in biology class, numb to the course material – numb because I'd discovered sex, so concentrating on anything else was hard.

The cafeteria was about as far away from the biology classroom as it was possible to be – three floors up, and located diagonally across the building. I stopped at my locker, threw my textbooks in like so much Burger King trash and was set to bolt for the caf, when Matt Gursky, this walking hairdo from *Youth Alive!*, buttonholed me.

"Jason, we need to talk."

"About what, Matt? I can't talk now. I'm in a hurry."

"Too much of a hurry to discuss the fate of your eternal soul?"

I looked at him. "You have sixty seconds. One, two, three, *go* . . ."

"I don't know if I like being treated like a – "

"Fifty-three, fifty-two, fifty-one . . ."

"Okay then, what's the deal with you and Cheryl?"

"The *deal*?"

"Yeah, the deal. The two of you. We know you've been having, or rather, you've been . . ."

"Been *what*?"

"You know. *Making it*."

"We have?"

"Don't deny it. *We've* been watching."

I'm a big guy. I'm big now, and I was big then. I took my left hand and clenched it around Matt's throat, my thumb on top of his voice box. I lifted him off the buffed linoleum and cracked the back of his head on a locker's ventilation slits. "Look, you meddlesome, sanctimonious cockroach . . ." I bounced him onto the floor, my knees locking his arms as surely as cast-iron shackles. "If you dare even hint, even one more time, that you or any other sexless, self-hating member of your Stasi goon squad have any [slug to the face] right to impose your ideas on my life, I'll come to your house in the dead of night, use a tire iron to smash your bedroom window and then obliterate your self-satisfied little pig face with it."

I stood up. "I hope I've made myself clear." I then walked away, toward the caf, climbing up flights of stairs, but I felt like I was walking on an airport's rubber conveyor belt.

I was maybe halfway across the middle floor when I heard sounds like popping fireworks, no big deal, because Halloween was coming up shortly. And then I noticed two grade nine students running past me, and then, some seconds later, dozens of students stumbling over themselves. One girl I knew, Tracy, who took over my paper route from me back in 1981, yelled at me there were three guys up in the cafeteria shooting students. She fled, and I remembered the ship turning upside down in *The Poseidon Adventure,* and the looks on the actors' faces as they clued into the fact that the ship was flipping: smashed champagne bottles, dying pianos, carved ice swans and people falling from the sky. The fire alarm went off.

Against the human stream, I rounded a stairwell – one with a mural of Maui or some other paradiselike place. The wall was pebble-finished and rubbed my right arm raw. At that point the alarm bell felt like crabs crawling on my head.

At the top of the stairs Mr. Kroger, an English teacher, stood with Miss Harmon, the principal's assistant, both looking besieged; life doesn't prepare you for high school massacres. When I tried to pass, Mr. Kroger said, "You're not going up there." Meanwhile, the gunshots were coming fast and furious around the corner and down the hall in the caf. Mr. Kroger said, "Jason, leave." The sprinklers kicked in. It was raining.

"Cheryl's in the cafeteria."

"Go. *Now*."

I grabbed his arm to move him away, but he toppled down the stairwell. *Oh, Jesus* – he went down like a box of junk falling from a top cupboard.

The shots from the caf continued. I ran toward the main foyer leading there. Bodies lay all around, like Halloween pumpkins smashed on the road on the morning of November first. I slowed down. Only one of the foyer's front windows hadn't been blasted out, and sprinkler water was picking up patches of light reflected from the trophy cases and the ceiling's fluorescents. Lori Kemper ran past. She was in the drama club and her arm was purple and was somehow no longer connected properly. On the linoleum was Layla Warner, not so lucky, in a disjointed heap by a trophy case. Two other students, equally bloody, ran by, and then there was this guy – Derek Something – lying in a red swirl of blood and sprinkler water, using his arms to drag himself away from the cafeteria doors. He croaked, "Don't go in there."

"Jesus, Derek." I grabbed him and hauled him back to the stairwell.

Inside the caf's glass doors I saw three of the school's younger loser gang wearing camouflage duck-hunting outfits. Two of them were arguing, pointing rifles at each other, while the third guy with a carbine looked on. Students were huddled under the banks of tables. If they were talking, I wasn't hearing anything, maybe because of the fire alarm and the sirens and helicopters outside. Once I entered the main foyer, what I remember is the silence in spite of the noise. In my head it might just as well have been a snowy day in the country.

I thought to myself, *Well, a rifle's a rifle. You can't go in there unarmed.* I scanned the immediate environment to find something, anything, I could use to kill a human being. The answer was just outside one of the blown-out windows: smooth gray rocks from the Capilano River, inside tree planters as a means keeping cigarette butts out of the soil. I walked out the window hole and saw riflemen and ambulances and a woman with a megaphone. Up the hill were hundreds of students, watching the events from behind cars; I could see their legs poking from below. I grabbed a river rock the size of a cantaloupe – it weighed as much as a barbell – and walked into the cafeteria. One of the gunmen lay in a heap on the floor, dead.

I yelled to the guy standing over him, "Put that gun down."

"What? You have got to be . . ."

He took a shot at me and missed. Then, in the best shot of my life, I estimated the distance between us, the mass of the rock, and the potential of my muscles. One, two, three, *pitch,* and the evil bastard was dead. Instantly dead, as I'd learn later. Justice.

And then I saw Cheryl. The carnage of the room was only now registering, the dead, the wounded, the red lakes by the vending machines. I climbed under a table and held Cheryl in my arms.

I whispered her name over and over, but her gaze only met mine once, before her head fell back, her eyes on the third gunman, who had been captured beneath a large, heavy tabletop. Students were now fighting each other for a place on top of the table, like people on the Berlin Wall in 1989, and then they all began to jump in unison, crushing the body like a Christmas walnut, one, two, THREE; one, two, THREE; and the distance between the tabletop and the floor shrank with each jump until finally, as I held Cheryl in my arms, the students – unbeknownst to the forces of the law outside – might just as well have been squishing mud between the floor and table.

*　　*　　*

It's a few minutes later, and I'm sitting shirtless on a smooth driftwood log that escaped from a boom up the coast. The air smells of mussel shoals, and Joyce and Brodie are in the low tide, chasing the long-suffering seagulls. The dogs seem able to amuse themselves without human intervention, which allows me to be expansive for a moment . . .

Okay, here's something which kind of ties into all this: one of my first memories. It's of my father, Reg, making me kneel on the staticky living room rug. I'd just been watching fireworks on the TV – it was the American bicentennial summer, 1976, so I was five. I'd been changing channels and lingered a microsecond too long, a game show where a rhinestoned blond "temptress" was showcasing a fridge-freezer set about to be won or lost. Reg, detecting lust/sin/temptation/evil, slapped the OFF button and then made me say a prayer for my future wife, "who may or may not yet be born." I had no idea what she was supposed to look like, so I asked Reg, whose response was to scoop me up and wallop the bejeezus out of me, after which he stormed out into his car and drove away, most likely to a men's religious discussion group he enjoyed bullying once a week. My mother peeked out the front window, turned around to me and said, "You know, dear, in the future, just think of an *angel*."

From then on, I could never look at a girl without wondering if *she* had been the target of my prayer, and the bellies of pregnant women counted, too. When I first saw Cheryl, in ninth grade, it was obvious that she was the antenna who'd been receiving my prayers. You just know these things. And when she became religious, that was my confirmation.

Sitting here on my log, I can feel women looking at me with the soul-seeking radar I once employed looking for my future wife. It's younger soccer-mom types mostly, married, here on the 'beach on a workday, frazzled from handling over-sugared toddlers cranky from too much sun. There are some teenage girls, too, but being on the far side of my twenties, I'm pretty much invisible to them. A blessing and a curse.

When I say I can *feel* women looking at me, I mean it in the sense of feeling hungry – you know you're hungry, but when you try to explain it, you can't. And it's as if I feel the thought rays of these women passing through me. But that sounds wrong. Maybe it's just lust. Maybe that's all it is.

The concession stand is down the beach, not far from where I'm sitting: Popsicles, fish & chips and onion burgers. Cheryl worked there in her last summer. She really loved it because there were no *Alive!* people there. I can see her point.

*   *   *

If you'd met me before the massacre, you'd think you'd just met a walking storage room full of my father's wingding theories and beliefs. That's assuming I even spoke to you, which I probably wouldn't have done, because I don't speak much. Until they put a chip in my brain to force me to speak, I plan to remain quiet.

If you'd met me just before the massacre, you'd have assumed I was statistically average, which I was. The only thing that made me different from most other people my age is that I was married. That's it.

I suppose that, given my father and my older brother, it was inevitable that I be plunked into *Youth Alive!* Individually its members could be okay, but with a group agenda, they could be goons. They, more than anything, are the reason I remained mute.

Dad was thrilled Kent was the local *Alive!* grand pooh-bah, and at dinner he liked nothing more than hearing Kent reel out statistics about conversions, witnessings and money-raisers. If they ever argued, it was over trivialities: Should a swimming pool used in rituals be the temperature of blood, or should it be as cold as possible, to add a dimension of discomfort? The answer: cold. Why miss an opportunity for joylessness?

Cheryl stayed for supper a few times at our house, and the meals were surprisingly uneventful. I kept on waiting for Dad to pull back a curtain to reveal a witch-dunking device, but he and Cheryl got on well, I suspect because she was a good listener and knew better than to interrupt my father. I wonder if Dad saw in Cheryl the kind of girl he thinks he ought to have married – someone who'd already been converted rather than someone he'd have to mold, and then psychologically torture, like my mother.

After our marriage, we all had dinner together just once, before Kent went back to school in Alberta. Kent and the Peeping Toms from *Alive!* were beginning to spy on us by then, and I've never really been sure whether Kent told Dad about Cheryl and me. If he had, it wouldn't have been with malice. It would have been Item Number 14 on the agenda, sandwiched between the need for more stacking chairs and the recitation of a letter from a starving waif in Dar es Salaam who received five bucks a month from the Klaasen family.

In any event, my father treated Cheryl and me more like children than adults, which felt patronizing to me. If he knew we were married, he'd treat us like man and woman instead of girl and boy. Because of that dinner, I knew I soon had soon to devise a way of announcing our marriage. I wanted a proper dinner in a restaurant, and Cheryl just wanted to phone a few people and leave it at that.

*   *   *

Joyce is a liquid snoring heap by my apartment's front window. It's not so much an apartment – it's more like a nest – but Joyce doesn't mind. I suppose, from a dog's perspective, a dirty apartment is far more interesting than one that's been heavily Windexed and vacuumed. Do I keep the place dirty to scare people away? No, I keep it dirty because Reg was a neat freak – cleanliness . . . godliness . . . pathetically predictable, I know. The only person I'd ever allow in here would be Reg, if only to torment him with my uncleanness. But then nothing on earth would make me invite Reg into any home of mine.

My answering machine tells me I have seven new calls – no loser, me! – but I know they're mostly going to be about

Kent's memorial service this evening. *Will I be there? Will I show up?* Yeah, sure, okay. I may be a disaster, but I'm not a write-off. Yet.

Of course, I'll be needing something clean to wear, and it's too late to haul my shirt pile to the dry cleaners, so I'll have to iron a dirty shirt, which is dumb, because it permanently bakes the crud into the fabric. I now have to go find the shirt, excavate the iron from under one of dozens of piles of crap, put water into it, and clear a spot on the floor to put the board up and – it's easier to write.

More about the massacre . . .

There was some lag time between when the third gunman, Duncan Boyle, was downed and when kids started leaving the caf. Even the kids closest to the door took a while to make the connection between gunlessness and freedom. If anything, students gravitated toward their killers' corpses, I think to make a visual confirmation of death. The alarms were still blaring, and the sprinklers were still raining on us, and there were just so *many* kids dripping with both blood and water.

I was glued to Cheryl. My arms actually made suction noises when I moved them. I was covered in her blood. All of her friends had gone. Freaks. When the mass exodus began from the caf, the authorities swooped in, in every conceivable form – police snipers, guys in balaclavas, firemen, ambulance workers – all too late. They were taking photos, putting up colored tape, and everyone was screaming to turn off the alarms and the sprinklers, as they were not merely annoying, but were contaminating the crime scene. For all I know, those sirens and sprinklers may still be on, as I've not returned to the building since that day.

"Son, stand up." It was an RCMP guy with the big RCMP moustache they're all issued once they earn their badge. Another cop looked at me and said, "That's the guy."

So apparently I had now become "the guy."

I should describe at this point what it's like to hold a dying person in your arms. The first thing is how quickly they cool off, like dinner on a plate. Second, you keep waiting for their face to come back to life, their eyes to open. Even with Cheryl cooling in my arms, I didn't really believe she was dead. So when an authority figure of proven uselessness told me to let go of the body of my wife, whose face I knew would reanimate momentarily, my reaction was to stick with my wife. "Go to hell."

"No, really, son, stand up."

"You heard me."

The other cop asked, "Is he giving you trouble, John?"

"Lay off, Pete. Can't you see he's . . . ?"

"What I can see is that he's tampering with a crime scene. You – get up. Now."

Pete wasn't worth responding to. I held Cheryl close. *The world is an ugly ugly ugly place.*

"Son, come on."

"Sir, I said *no*."

"Pete, I don't know what to do. She's dead. Let him hold her."

"No. And if he keeps it up, you know what to do."

"Actually, I don't."

I tuned them out. From my vantage point, soggy reddened lunch bags and backpacks lay everywhere; the wounded were being removed with the same speed and efficiency that coliseum staff remove chairs after a concert.

Underneath Cheryl I saw her notebook, festooned with its ballpoint scribbles: GOD IS NOWHERE/GOD IS NOW HERE; GOD IS NOWHERE/GOD IS NOW HERE. I didn't give it any thought past that. A man's arm reached down and tried to tug my arms away from her, but I flinched and held on. Then a dozen arms reached in. *Pow,* I became a one-man supernova, firing my legs in all directions, refusing to let go of Cheryl, but they managed to pull us apart, and that was the last time I touched her. Within forty-eight hours she was embalmed, and for reasons that will follow, I wasn't permitted to attend her funeral.

Once they'd pulled me away from Cheryl, they shoved me into the foyer and then promptly forgot me. And so I walked through the same shot-out empty window frame as before and onto the front plaza, where it was sunny and bright. I remembered this thing Cheryl once said, how God sees no difference between night and day, how God only sees the sun at the center and the greater plan, and that night and day were merely human distinctions. I figured I now understood her point, except that for me, I didn't see any greater plan.

*   *   *

I won my apartment in a poker game, from Dennis, a concrete pourer who'll spend the rest of his life losing his apartments in poker games. He's that kind of guy. The place is nicer than something I would have found on my own; I even have a balcony the size of a card table, which I've managed to ruin with failed houseplants and empty bottles that will someday enter the downstairs recycling bins. It looks out on the rear of small shops on Marine Drive, and beyond that to English Bay – the Pacific – and the rest of the city across the bay.

I checked my messages. The first was from Les, reminding me to bring the nail gun for tomorrow's job, which is framing in a towel cabinet for a real estate tycoon's fantasy bathroom. The second message was from Chris, Cheryl's brother, saying that he can't risk leaving the U.S. for tonight's memorial because if they catch him either coming or going across the border, that's the end of his visa, which he needs to design spreadsheets, whatever they are, down in Redwood City, wherever that is. The third was from my mother, saying she didn't think she could handle the memorial. The fourth was her again, saying that she thought she could. The fifth call was a hang-up with five seconds of bar noise. The sixth was Nigel, a contractor buddy from a recent project who doesn't yet know I'm a living monkey's paw, asking me if I want to shoot some pool tonight. Soon enough Nigel will learn about my "story," and then he'll go buy a cheapo massacre exploitation paperback in some second-hand bookstore. His behavior around me will change: he'll walk on eggshells, and then he'll want to discuss life after death, crop circles, gun laws, Nostradamus or stuff along those lines, and then I'll have to drop him as a friend because he'll know way more about me than anyone ought to know, and the imbalance is, as I age, more of a pain than anything else. I don't want or need it.

Call seven is my mother again, asking me to phone her. I do.

"Mom."

"Jason."

"You feeling weird about tonight?"

"Someone has to take care of the twins. I thought maybe I could take the twins off Barb's hands for the evening."

"Kent's friends have probably sorted that out weeks ago. You know what they're like."

"I guess so."

"How about I drive you."

"Could you?"

"Sure."

*   *   *

Okay.

After leaving the cafeteria, I walked out onto the sunlit concrete plaza, where I turned around and saw myself reflected in the one remaining unshot window, and I was all one color, purple. Gurneys with their oxygen masks and plasma trees covered the front plaza like blankets on a beach. I saw bandages being applied so quickly they had bits of autumn leaves trapped inside the weave. I remember a sheet being pulled over the face of this girl, Kelly, who was my French class vocabulary partner. She didn't look shot at all, but she was dead.

There were seagulls flying above – rare for that altitude, and –

Well, I've seen all the photos a million times like everyone else, but they just don't capture the way it felt to be there – the sunlight and the redness of the blood: that's always cropped out of magazines, and this bugs me because when you crop the photo, you tell a lie.

I was thinking, *Okay. I guess I should just go home and wash up and get on with things.* Up the hill, hundreds of students were being held back by police barricades. When I looked to my left, a medic plunged a syringe like a railway spike into the chest of a friend of mine, Demi Harshawe. A few steps away, an attendant running with a plasma tree tripped over a varsity coat soaked in coagulating blood.

In my pocket I felt my car keys, and I thought, *If I can just find my car, I'll be able to leave here, and everything will be just fine.* When I walked down to the auxilary lot where I'd parked that day, nobody stopped me. I'd later learn that I'd accidentally fallen through every crack in the security system, which was for a time interpreted as having *sneaked* through every crack in the system. Regardless, nobody called my name, and, by the way, those grief counselors they always talk about on TV? Oh, come *on*.

I was headed for my car, but then I saw Cheryl's white Chevette – it looked so warm in the sunlight, and I just wanted to be near it and feel warmth from it, so I went and lay down on the hood. The sun was indeed warm, in that feeble October way, and I curled up on the car's hood, leaving red rusty finger-painting swishes, then fell into whatever it is that isn't sleep but isn't wakefulness, either.

A hand shook me, and when I opened my eyes, the sun was a bit further to the west. It was two RCMP officers, one with a German shepherd, and the other with a rifle speaking into a headset: "He's alive. Not injured, we don't think. Yeah, we'll hold him."

I blinked and looked at the men. I was no longer "the guy"; I was now merely "him." I tried lifting my right arm, but the blood had bonded it to the hood. It made a ripping-tape sound as I pulled it away. My clothes felt made of plasticine. I asked, "What time is it?"

The officers stared at me as if their dog had just spoken to them. "Just after two o'clock," one of them said.

I didn't know what to say or ask. *What was the grand*

total? I blanked, and two very nice-seeming women ran down to the lot toward us carrying large red plastic medical boxes.

"Are you shot?"

"No."

"Cut?"

"No."

"Have you been drinking alcohol or using drugs?"

"No."

"Are you on any medications?"

"No."

"Allergies?"

"Novocaine."

"Is the blood on your body from a single source?"

"Uh – yes."

"Do you know the name of the person?"

"Cheryl Anway."

"Did you know Cheryl Anway?"

"Uh – yes. Of *course* I did. Why do you need to know that?"

"If we know the relationship then we can more precisely evaluate you for stress or shock."

"That makes sense." I felt more logical than I had any right to be.

"Then did you know Cheryl Anway?"

"She's my . . . girlfriend."

My use of the present tense flipped a switch. The women looked at the RCMP officers, who said, "He was sleeping on the hood."

"I wasn't asleep."

They looked at me.

"I don't know *what* I was doing, but it wasn't sleep."

One of the women asked, "Is this Cheryl's car?"

"Yeah." I stood up. The fire alarms were still clanging, and the concertlike sensation of thousands of people nearby was distinct.

The other female medic said, "We can give you something to calm you down."

"Yes. Please."

Alcohol chilled a patch of skin on my left shoulder and I felt the needle go in.

*   *   *

Like anyone, I've seen those movies about army barracks life where evil drill sergeants, with cobra venom for spinal fluid, sentence privates to six years of latrine duty for an improperly folded bedsheet corner. But unlike most people, I have to leave the theater or switch the channel because it reminds me of my life as a child.

You're nothing, you hear me? Nothing. You're not even visible to God. You're not even visible to the devil. You are zero.

Here's another thought from the mind and mouth of Reg: *You are a wretch. You are a monster and you are weak and you will be passed over in the great accounting.* As can be clearly seen, my father's primary tactic was to nullify my existence. Maybe today's banking adventure with zeroes stems from that.

Kent, however, was never *nothing*. At the very least, he was always expected to join my father's insurance firm after college – which he did – get married to a suitable girl – which he did – and lead a proud and righteous life – which he did, until exactly one year ago, when a teenager in a Toyota

Celica turned him into a human casserole up by the Exit 5 off-ramp near Caulfeild.

I miss Kent, but God, I wish he and I had been genuinely close as opposed to Don't-they-look-nice-together-in-the-airbrushed-family-portrait close. He was always so bloody organized, and his efforts at all activities always made my own efforts pale. Kent was also righteous; he was sent home from school in sixth grade for speaking up against Easter egg hunts (pagan; trivializes God; symbols of fertility that secretly promote lust). Granted, lust is purely theoretical in grade six, but he knew how to spin things the *Alive!* way. He was a born politician.

Dad left scorch marks behind him as he jetted off to the school's offices that pre-Easter afternoon, of course to take Kent's side. Through bullying and threat of litigation (he was an imposing, hawklike man), he was able to get Easter egg making banned in Kent's classroom. The school caved simply because they wanted a demented nutcase out of their way. That night at dinner, there was extra praying, and Kent and Dad discussed Easter egg paganism in detail, way too far over my head. As for my mother, she might as well have been watching the blue-white snows of Channel 1.

Here's another thought, this one about Reg: when I was maybe twelve, I got caught plundering the neighbors' raspberry patch. Talk about sin. For the weeks that followed, my father pointedly pretended I didn't exist. He'd bump into me in the hallway and say nothing, as if I were a chair. Kent the politician always stayed utterly neutral during this sort of conflict.

The bonus of being invisible was that if I didn't exist, I also couldn't be punished. This played itself out mostly at the dinner table. My mother (on her sixth glass of Riesling from the spigot of a two-liter plastic-lined cardboard box) would ask how my woodwork assignment was going. I'd reply something like, "Reasonably well, but you know what?"

"What?"

"There's this rumor going around the school right now."

"Really?"

"Yeah. Word has it that God smokes cigarettes."

"Jason, please don't . . ."

"Also, and this is so weird, God drinks *and* he uses drugs. I mean, he invented the things. But the funny thing is, he's exactly the same drunk as sober."

Mom recognized the pattern. "Jason, let it rest." Kent sat there waiting for the crunch.

Taunting my father was possibly the one time where I became vocal. Here's another example: "It turns out God hates every piece of music written after the year 1901." The thing that really got to Dad was when I dragged God into the modern world.

"I hear God approves of various brands of cola competing in the marketplace for sales dominance."

Silence.

"I hear that God has a really bad haircut."

Silence.

During flu season and the week of my annual flu shot: "I hear that God allows purposefully killed germs to circulate in his blood system to fend off living germs."

Silence.

"I hear that if God were to drive a car, he'd drive a 1973 Ford LTD Brougham sedan with a claret-colored vinyl roof . . . with leather upholstery and an opera window."

"Would the thief please pass the margarine?"

I existed again.

*   *   *

It's midnight and Kent's memorial is over. Did I make it there? Yes. And I managed to pull my act together, and wore a halfway respectable suit, which I cologned into submission. But first I packed Joyce in the truck, and we drove to fetch Mom from her little condo at the foot of Lonsdale – a mock-Tudor space module built a few years ago, equipped with a soaker tub, optical fiber connections to the outer world and a fake wishing well in the courtyard area. Everyone else in the complex has kids; once they learned that Mom is indifferent to kids and baby-sitting – and that maybe she drinks too much – they shunned her. When I got there she was watching *Entertainment Tonight* while a single-portion can of Campbell's low-sodium soup caramelized on the left rear element. I sent it hissing into the sink.

"Hey, Mom."

"Jason."

I sat down, while Mom gave Joyce a nice rub. She said, "I don't think I can make it tonight, dear."

"That's okay. I'll let you know how it goes."

"It's a beautiful evening. Warm."

"It is."

She looked out the sliding doors. "I might go sit on the patio. Catch the last bit of sun."

"I'll come join you."

"No. You go."

"Joyce can stay with you tonight."

Mom and Joyce perked up at this. Joyce loves doing Mom duty: being a Seeing Eye dog is in her DNA, and in the end,

I'm not that much of a challenge for her. Mom fully engages Joyce's need to be needed, and I let them be.

It was a warm night, August, the only guaranteed-good-weather month in Vancouver. Even after the sun set, its light would linger well into the evening. The trees and shrubs along the roadside seemed hot and fuzzy, as if microwaved, and the roads were as clean as any in a video game. On the highway, the airborne pollen made the air look saliva syrupy, yet it felt like warm sand blowing on my arm. It struck me that this was exactly the way the weather was the night Kent was killed.

As I headed toward Exit 2, it also struck me that I would have to pass Exit 5 on the way to Barb's house. I rounded the corner, and there was my father, kneeling on the roadside in a wrinkled (I noticed even at seventy miles an hour) sinless black suit. My father: born of a Fraser Valley Mennonite family of daffodil farmers who apparently weren't strict enough for him, so he forged his own religious path, marching purse-lipped through the 1970s, so lonely and screwed up he probably nearly gave himself cancer from stress. He met my mother, who worked in a Nuffy's Donuts franchise in the same minimall as the insurance firm that employed him, calculating the likelihood and time of death of strangers. Mom was a suburban child from the flats of Richmond, now Vancouver's motherland of Tudor condominium units. Her shift at the donut shop overlapped Dad's by three hours. I know that at first she found Dad's passion and apparent clarity attractive – Mother Nature is cruel indeed – and I imagine my father found my mother a blank canvas onto which he could spew his gunk.

I pulled over to watch him pray. This was about as

interested as I'd been in praying since 1988. I could barely see my father's white Taurus parked back from the highway, on a street in the adjoining suburb, beside a small stand of Scotch broom. The absence of any other car on the highway made his presence seem like that of a soul in pilgrimage. That poor dumb bastard. He'd scared or insulted away or betrayed all the people who otherwise ought to have been in his life. He's a lonely, bitter, prideful crank, and I really have to laugh when I consider the irony that I've become, of course, the exact same thing. Memo to Mother Nature: *Thanks*.

*　　*　　*

From the high school's parking lot I was driven home sitting on a tarp in the police cruiser's rear seat, no sirens. When I walked in the door off the kitchen, my mother shrieked. I could see a Kahlúa bottle by the cheese grater, so I knew she was already looped; I'm sure the cops knew right away, too.

Mom hadn't been watching TV or listening to the radio, so my appearance at the kitchen door, laminated with a deep maroon muck, had to have been a shock. I just wanted to get the stuff off me, so I kissed her, said I was fine and allowed the cops to bring her up-to-date. In the slipstream of the sedative injection I'd been given back in the parking lot I felt clear-minded and calm. Far too calm. As I was changing out of my bloodied clothes, what passed through my mind was – of all things – curiosity as to how my mother filled her days. I had no idea. She had no job and was stranded amid the mountainside's suburban Japanese weeping maples and mossy roofs. Greater minds have gone mad from the level of boredom she endured. By the time I was seventeen, her once communicative Reg conversed solely with a God so demanding that of all the people on Earth, only he – and possibly Kent – had any chance of making heaven. Just a few years ago my mother said to me during a lunch, "Just *imagine* how it must feel to know that your family won't be going to heaven with you – I mean, truly *believing* that. We're ghosts to him. We might as well be dead."

As I disrobed for the shower, flecks of blood flittered onto the bathroom's gold linoleum. I bundled up my clothes and tossed them out the window onto the back patio, where, I learned later, raccoons pilfered them in the night. I showered, and my thoughts were almost totally focused on how cool and sensible the medic's injection had made me. I could have piloted and landed a 747 on that stuff. And with a newly minted junkie's bloodless logic, I was already trying to figure out how soon I could locate more, and at least I had something else to focus on besides Cheryl's death.

When I walked back into the living room, the TV was on. Mom was transfixed, and the RCMP officers were on walkie-talkies, the phone – you name it. Mom grabbed my hand and wouldn't let me go, and I saw for the first time the helicopter and news service images that trail me to this day, images I have yet to fully digest. My mother's grip was so hard that I noticed my fingers turning white. I still wonder how things might have gone without that delicious injection.

"We need to ask your son some questions, ma'am."

Reg walked in from the carport door just then. "Son?"

"I'm okay, Dad."

He looked at me, and his face seemed – for reasons that will become evident soon enough – annoyed. "Well then. Good. Mrs. Elliot at the school said you'd been taken away unhurt."

An officer said, "We have to question your son, sir."

Mom wailed, "Cheryl's dead . . ."

"Why do you need to question Jason?"

"Procedure, sir."

"Jason, why are they questioning you?"

"You tell me."

Mom said, "Didn't you hear me?"

Dad ignored Mom, and by extension, Cheryl. "What does my son have to do with any of this?"

"He was right there in the cafeteria," said one cop. "If he hadn't thrown that rock, who knows how many more fatalities there might have been."

"Rock?"

"Yes. Your son's quick thinking – "

The other cop cut in, "That boulder killed the main gunman."

"Gun*man*? He was fifteen, tops."

Dad turned to me. "You killed a boy today?"

A cop said, "He's a hero, sir."

"Jason, did you kill a boy today?"

"Uh-huh."

"Did you intend to kill him?"

"Yeah, I did. Would you rather have had him shoot me?"

"That's not what I asked you. I asked if you intended to kill him."

"Mr. Klaasen," the first cop said. "Perhaps you don't understand, your son's actions saved the lives of dozens of students."

Reg looked at him. "What I understand is that my son experienced murder in his heart and chose not to rise above that impulse. I understand that my son is a murderer."

While he was saying this, the TV screen was displaying the death and injury statistics. The cops didn't know how to respond to Reg's – my *father's* – alien logic. I looked over at my mother, who was by no means a slight woman. I saw her grab one of a pair of massive lava rock lamps, shockingly ugly and astoundingly heavy. Mom picked up the lamp by its tapered top, and with all her force whapped it sidelong into Reg's right kneecap, shattering it into twenty-nine fragments that required a marathon eighteen-hour surgery and seven titanium pins to rectify – and here's the good part: the dumb bastard had to wait two days for his operation because all the orthopedic surgeons were busy fixing massacre victims. *Ha!*

My mom, bless her, kicked into full operatic mode: "*Crawl* to your God, you arrogant bastard. See if your God doesn't look at the slime trail you leave behind you and throw you to the buzzards. You heartless, sad little man. You don't even have a soul. You killed it years ago. I want you to die. You got that? I want you to *die*."

An ambulance was summoned to squire my screaming father to emergency. The police never officially reported the incident, nor did Reg. But in that one little window of time, many lasting decisions were made. First, any love for my father that might have remained either in my mother's heart or my own – vaporized. Second, we knew for sure that Dad was unfixably nuts. Third, upon discharge a few weeks later, he was coolly shipped off to his sister's daffodil ranch in the most extreme eastern agricultural reaches of the city, in Agassiz, a soggy and spooky chunk of property surrounded by straggly alders, blackberry brambles, dense firs, pit bulls, Hell's Angels drug labs and an untold number of bodies buried in unmarked graves.

But my parents never got divorced. Dad always paid support and . . . who knows what ever really goes on inside a relationship. Dad probably felt guilty for wrecking Mom's life. No. that would imply feeling on his part.

*   *   *

I arrived at Barb's house a bit on the late side. The attendees were mostly Kent's friends – friends who'd seemed old to me in high school and who always will. Folding wooden chairs were arranged on the back lawn, none of them level; the forest, after decades of lying in wait, was silently sucking the old ranch house and the moss-clogged lawn back into the planet. The twins (that would be *you,* my nephews) and a few other babies were in the TV room, being as quiet and gentle as their pious parents, as they were serenaded by a tape of soothing nature sounds: waves lapping a Cozumel beach; birds of the Guyana rain forest; rain falling in an Alaskan fjord.

Kent's friends had all been hardcore *Youth Alive!*ers who'd never strayed, who became dentists and accountants and moved to Lynn Valley along with most of the city's Kents. I'd seen none of them in the year since Kent's funeral. I knew they'd all enjoy a righteous tingle from any confirmation of my life's downwardly sloping line. My slapped-together ensemble delivered the goods.

"Hey, Barb."

"Finally, somebody from your family shows up."

"Mom can't make it. One guess why. Reg is praying up by Exit 5. I imagine he'll creak his way here soon enough."

"Lovely."

I poured myself a glass of red wine; piety mercifully ended at the bar with this crowd.

Barb was never involved with *Youth Alive!*, and because of this, had always felt like an outsider in the Kent set. As I looked out at all the healthy teeth and hair on the patio, I realized how sad and insufficient any memorial service would be. I missed Kent. Badly. "Was the service your idea, Barb?"

"Yes, but not this big Hollywood production. They're trying to set me up with some guy in the group. It's so clinical and mechanical." She looked out onto the lawn. "They're pretty efficient. I have to hand that to them. All I had to do was open the door and look wounded."

"Charitable."

"Stick a potato in it. Your job, by the way, is to continue being the doomed loser brother. It shouldn't be a stretch."

"And your job?"

"Stoic widow who at least has two kids as a souvenir."

I went out to the car and brought in a canvas duffel bag filled with some presents for the two of you, but your mother got mad at me for spoiling you, a battle that will never stop, because I'll never stop spoiling you. I went in to see you in your cribs – chubby, a bit of curly hair, Kent's smile, which is actually my mother's smile. I gave you each some animal puppets and entertained you with them for a while.

Out on the patio, I shook a few hands and tried not to look like a doomed loser. Kent's friends were using the technically friendly *Youth Alive!* conversation strategy with me. Example: "That's *great*, Jason, Gina and I were thinking of redoing the guest bathroom, *weren't we*, Gina?"

"Oh yeah. We really *were*. We ought to take down your phone number."

"We'll get it from you after the service."

"*Great.*"

After a few minutes of this, Gary, Kent's best friend, tinkled his glass and the group sat down. On easels up front were color photocopy enlargements of Kent's life: Kent white-water rafting; Kent at a cigar party; Kent playing Frisbee golf; Kent and Barb lunching in a Cabo San Lucas patio bistro; Kent at his stag party, pretending to drink a yard-long glass of beer. Each of these photos emphasized the absence of similar photos in my own life.

Gary began giving a speech, which I tuned out, and when it felt as if it was nearing the end, I heard a click behind me: Reg trying to open the latch on the living room's sliding doors. Barb got up, offered a terse hello, brought him down onto the lawn and gave him a chair. We all remembered Kent for a silent minute, which was hard for me. Kent's death meant that there were more Jasons in the world than there were Kents, an imbalance I don't like. I'm not sure whether I'm any good for the world.

I sprang up when the minute of silence ended, and dashed to the bar in the kitchen. There was nothing hard there, just wine; chugging was in order, so I poured most of a bottle of white into a twenty-ounce *Aladdin* souvenir plastic drinking cup, then downed it like Gatorade after a soccer game. Barb saw me do this and spoke in a sarcastic Dick and Jane tone: "Gosh, Jason – you must be very thirsty."

"Yes, I am, Barb." She let it go. Outside, all of Kent's friends were doing Dad duty, fine by me. I asked Barb if she ever spoke with Reg these days.

"No."

"Never?"

"Never."

I decided to be naughty. "You should try."

"Why on *earth* would I want to do that?"

"Jesus, Barb. It's Kent's memorial. You have to do something." This was not strictly true, but I'd pushed a guilt button.

"You're right."

She went outside and joined a trio of Kent's friends with Reg. I stood nearby so I could hear their conversation.

Barb said, "Reg, I'm glad you could come."

"Thank you for inviting me."

Barb turned to Kent's friends. "What were you guys talking about?"

"Cloning."

Barb said, "This Dolly-the-sheep thing must be raising a few eyebrows."

One friend, whose name was Brian, said, "You better believe it." He asked my father, "Reg, do you think a clone would have the same soul as its parent, or perhaps have a new one?"

"A clone with a soul?" Dad rubbed his chin. "No. I don't think it would be possible for a clone to have a soul."

"No soul? But it would be a living human being. How could it not . . . ?"

"It would be a monster."

Another friend, Riley, cut in here: "But then what about your twin grandsons? They're identical, so when the embryo splits, technically, one nephew is the clone of the other. You think that one of them has a soul and one doesn't?"

Barb, trying to lighten things, said, "Talk about monsters – if I miss feeding time by even three minutes, then I become Ripley, and they become the Alien."

Reg wrecked this attempt at cheeriness. He'd obviously been thinking hard, his face sober like a bust of Abraham Lincoln. "Yes," he said, "I think you might have to consider the possibility that one of the boys might not have a soul."

Silence. All the real smiles turned fake.

"You're joking," said Riley.

"Joking? About the human soul? Never."

Barb turned abruptly and walked away. The three guys stood there looking at Reg. Then Barb returned with one of the wooden folding chairs, holding it sideways like a tennis racket.

"You evil, evil bastard. Never ever come back to this house, ever."

"Barb?"

"Go now. Because I'll break you in two. I will."

"Is this really – "

"Don't go meek on me now, you sadistic bastard."

I'd seen this side of Barb before and knew she would push this situation way further if she wanted to. Riley made some gesture to stand between her and my father. I went over to Barb and tried removing the chair from her grip, but she clutched it using every sinew she'd developed as captain of the girls' field hockey team.

"Barb. No."

"You heard what he said."

"He's not worth the effort."

"He should die for the things he's done to people. Some-one has to stop him."

I looked at my father, into his eye slits, and knew that nothing had changed, that he had no real understanding of what he'd done to deserve this. I would have poured the remains of my wine on him, but that would have been a waste.

Barb said, "I'll pour Drāno on your grave, you sick bastard."

Reg took the hint. Some of the wives (not a girlfriend in the bunch) accompanied my father to his car.

I sat with your mother while the *Alive!* crew scoured the house of memorial residue. I said, "Barb, you never believed me about Reg, about how evil he is. Now you know."

"It's one thing to hear about it, Jason. And another to see it in operation."

"Barb, the thing about Dad is that he'll always betray you in the end. Even if you think you've gotten close to him, earned your way into his bosom the way Kent did, in the end he'll always sell you out to his religion. He's actually a pagan that way – he has to make sacrifices, so he sacrificed his family one by one. Tonight he offered the twins to his God. If he were a dog, I'd shoot him."

And so I picked up Joyce at Mom's where the TV station had kicked into late-night infomercials. She was sleeping it off on the couch. I drove home and I'm going to bed soon.

* * *

I arrived at Ambleside Beach a few minutes ago, and something unusual happened. I was sitting in the truck's cab removing a burr from Joyce's flank, while looking at my stack of pink invoice papers, when this pleasant-enough woman in a purple fleece coat, holding a baby in her arms, comes up to the window and says, "Homework?"

Now, if I met you last week, I'll never remember your name, but if we went through kindergarten together, you're still in my brain for good: "Demi Harshawe!" Demi is the massacre victim I'd last seen on October 4, 1988, having a silver spike jabbed into her unclothed heart.

"How are you doing, Jason?"

"No surprises. You?" Joyce trampled over my lap to lick Demi's face.

"Pretty average, I guess. I got married two summers ago. My last name is Minotti now. This here's Logan." Joyce dragged her tongue right across Logan's face.

"Sorry."

"It's okay. We're a dog family. See – Logan didn't mind it one bit."

"It's so great to see you."

We were both six again, and I felt so innocent and genuinely free, like we'd just quit jobs we hated. After maybe five minutes I asked Demi about her health – she'd been one of the kids shot over by the vending machines, and she'd lost a foot.

"I don't even notice it anymore. I do Pilates three times a week and coach softball with my sister. To be honest, wearing braces back in elementary school was way harder to deal with. How about you?"

Demi knew, in the way everyone knows, about how things went wrong for me in the weeks after the massacre. We're both ten years older, too, so I could describe things to her in non-candy-coated terms. "You know what? I never got over Cheryl. Not ever. I doubt I will. I try really hard to join the real world, but it never seems to work, and lately I think I've stopped trying, which scares me more than anything. I do house renovations on a by-the-hour basis and all my friends are barflies."

She thought this over for a second. "I stopped trusting

people, too, after the shootings, and until I met my husband, Andreas, I didn't think I'd ever trust people again. And for what it's worth, I think you're one of the few people I could trust, now that I believe in trust again."

"Thanks."

"No, thank *you*. After all the junk you had to go through." Demi paused for a second. "I was in the hospital for two weeks after the massacre. I missed all those hand-holding ceremonies and flowers and services and teddy bears et cetera. I really regret that, because maybe it would have made me a better person – or at least maybe I wouldn't go around looking at everybody as evil instead of good."

"I doubt it."

Demi sighed. "When I talk like this, Andreas thinks I'm coldhearted. But then he wasn't there. We were. And if you weren't, you weren't."

We'd hit on something irreducible here, and talking much beyond this point would have felt like a betrayal of our shared memories. We made our quick good-byes, and Demi and Logan headed down to the water, and here I am now in my truck's cab, the scribbler of Ambleside Beach.

*   *   *

It's an hour later and I'm still sitting in the truck.

I wish I could be as innocent as I was at six, the way I felt just briefly while talking with Demi, but that's childish. I wish humans were better than we are, but we're not. I wish I knew *how* bad I could become. I wish I could get a printout that showed me exactly how susceptible I was to a long list of sins. Gluttony: 23 percent susceptible. Envy: 68 percent susceptible. Lust: 94 percent susceptible. That kind of thing.

Oh God, it's religion all over again; it's my father's corrosive bile percolating through my soil and tickling my taproot. Be as pious as you want, people are slime, or, as my father might say, we're all slime *in the eyes of God.* It's the same thing. And even if you decided to fight the evil, to attain goodness or religious ecstasy, not much really changes. You're still stuck being *you,* and *you* was pretty much decided long before you started asking these questions.

Maybe clones are the way out of all of this. If Reg is against them, that means they're probably a good idea. And as a clone, you pop off the assembly line with an owner's manual written by the previous *you* – a manual as helpful as the one that accompanies a 1999 VW Jetta. Imagine all the crap this would save you – the wasted time, the hopeless dreams. I'm going to really think about this: an owner's manual for *me.*

*   *   *

It's midnight. I cut short my evening with my barfly construction buddies. We shot a few buckets of balls at the Park Royal driving range, then had a few beers, but I just couldn't bring myself to continue. Writing this document has taken a firm grip of me.

Here's an overview of what happened after the Delbrook Massacre.

The fact that I'd never met the three gun wielders didn't seem to matter. In published transcripts of interviews with the police, on the morning of the event I was "agitated." I walked "cavalierly" out of chem class without so much as a nod to the teacher. I was seen having an "emotional confrontation" with Cheryl. I "assaulted, drew blood from, and gave a concussion to" Matt Gursky from *Youth Alive!* I also assaulted Mr. Kroger "with seeming forethought," and I "seemingly knew to enter the cafeteria just after Cheryl Anway had been shot."

I think the public was desperate for cause and effect. At first glance, I suppose I'd probably be suspicious of me, too, and I'm pretty sure it was my father's bizarre reaction to the news that got police to thinking about me – from a hero to a suspect. Whatever the cause, the morning after the shootings I saw my yearbook photo on the front of the paper with the headline MASTERMIND?

The only thing missing was motive. The three nutcases with guns were screwed-up geeks lost in a stew of paranoia, role-playing games, military dreams and sexual rejection. They were a slam-dunk. With me, the case seemed to revolve around my relationship with Cheryl, about the fight we had that morning and reasons why I might want her dead. The best police minds couldn't engineer a reason no matter how soap-operatic their thinking.

On my side, I refused to make my life with Cheryl anybody's business but my own. I didn't mention our marriage because it was sacred; I wasn't going to let the massacre make it profane. I refused to let it be used as some kind of plot twist in the final five minutes of an episode of *Perry Mason*. So I said nothing, only that Cheryl wanted to talk about feelings, and I didn't. As simple as that. Which is basically what it was.

*　　*　　*

Okay, I'm not lying here, but I'm not disclosing everything. Truth is, Cheryl had just found out she was pregnant. That was what we'd been discussing at her locker. I was so taken aback by the news that I said something stupid, I forget what, and then I told her I had to prepare equipment for a Junior A team. Me – a *father* – and all I can say is "I have to get stuff ready for the Junior A team."

Even the idea of the baby got lost in the ordeal of the first two weeks. It wasn't until a month later, while I was waiting for a bus in New Brunswick, the temperature well below zero, that the baby caught up to me. I had to go behind a cedar hedge to cry. My nose began to bleed from the dry air, and the blood brought even more . . . Well, you get the picture.

As a result of the baby, I began doing what I used to do, wondering which woman was going to be my wife – except that now I looked at every child I saw and wondered if he or she was supposed to be mine. And then for a while I couldn't be near kids at all, and I got jobs up the coast in logging camps, construction and surveying.

And now? And now I guess I'll continue writing about the aftermath of the massacre. My many friends from *Youth Alive!* set the tone, gleefully providing police with a McCarthy-era dossier on Cheryl and me – a diary of the time we spent together after we returned from Las Vegas. The entries describe everything but the sex: where the cars were parked; what rooms were used and which lights went on and off at what time; the state of our clothing and hair before and after; the expressions on our faces – most often variations on the theme of "satisfied."

News that the police had taken me away from the parking lot caused rumors to quickly spread. By evening our house had been egged and paint-bombed. The police had cordoned it off, and advised us that it would probably be easier and safer if I spent the night at the station and Mom found a hotel or motel room.

Kent flew in from Edmonton. He was in his second year at the University of Alberta, working toward a CPA degree. Having Dad in the hospital was a blessing, as I at least didn't have to worry about him selling me further down the river. He and Mom, in their last act of married unity, synchronized their stories about the fractured knee, and then called it quits. I wish I could have been a fly on the wall for *that* little chat.

My main memories of those two weeks when I was under suspicion are of moving from one spartanly furnished room to another – a cell, a motel room or an interrogation room. I was what you'd now call a person of interest, living in a legal netherworld, neither free nor in custody. I remember eating mostly takeout Chinese or pizza, and having to hide in the bathroom when it was delivered. I remember always having to dial 9 before phone calls to my lawyer, and there was this chestnut-colored kiss-curl wig given to me by a woman from the RCMP. I was to wear it when we drove from place to place, but no matter how many times we rinsed it, it smelled like a thrift store. Potential angry mobs or not, it was stupid and I chucked it in the trash. There was this one interrogation room that smelled like cherry cola, and everywhere, the same yearbook photos being endlessly recycled on TV and in the papers.

I remember coming back from a questioning session one morning to find my mother opening the motel door with a large vodka stain shaped like Argentina on her blouse. And I wondered if I'd need to take a death certificate to Nevada to become officially unmarried. Is there even a name for this – "widowered" sounds wrong.

I ate chocolate bars from the Texaco for breakfast. Kent

and I drove once to the cemetery where Cheryl had been buried, but there were TV vans, so we didn't go in. All over the embankment beside the police station I saw magic mushrooms sprouting, which seemed funny to me. And I remember Kent returning from the house where he'd gone to clean up the eggs and paint, and how he refused to discuss it.

One thing Kent did during this time was, as ever, not take sides. He never said it in so many words, but he spent hours on the phone with *Alive!*ers and could only have been placating them.

"They think I organized it, don't they?"

"They're curious and angry like everybody else."

"But they do."

"They're just confused. Let it go. You'll be cleared soon enough."

"Do you think I was involved?"

Kent waited half a second too long to answer this. "No."

"You *do*."

"Jason, let it ride."

The thought of my brother not really being on my side frightened me so much that I did let it ride.

In any event, I remember the days becoming shorter, and Halloween approaching, and chipping my tooth on the police station drinking fountain.

One further thing I remember was Mom going on a Nostradamus kick. She was trying to find the massacre foretold in his prophecies somewhere. As if.

Hey Nostradamus! Did you predict that once we found the Promised Land we'd all start offing each other? And did you predict that once we found the Promised Land, it would be the final Promised Land, and there'd never be another one again? And if you were such a good clairvoyant, why didn't you just write things straight out? What's with all the stupid rhyming quatrains? Thanks for nothing.

But most of all I remember making sure that I got my injection every day right on time, at noon and midnight. After I got it, I had a five-minute window when I didn't have to think about Cheryl, alive, dying or dead.

I'm drunk.

*   *   *

And now I'm hung over. It's morning and it's raining outside, the first rain in a month. I think I'll skip working on the built-in towel rack for the day. Les will tell the client I'm at another job. That's the price he pays for having a drinking buddy on twenty-four-hour call.

I was going to do an owner's manual to myself, or rather, my future clone. Now's as good a time as any.

Dear Clone . . .
It's you speaking. Or rather it's me, but with a helluva lot more mileage on me than you have, so just trust me, okay? Where to start . . . Okay, as far as bodies go, you lucked out in most respects. Around the age of seventeen you'll hit six foot one, and you'll be neither skinny nor given to fat. You'll be left-handed and bad with numbers but pretty good with words. You'll be allergic to any molecule that ends with the suffix "-aine," meaning benzocaine, novocaine, and, most important, *cocaine*. I learned this when getting a filling in third grade. If I'd been able to do cocaine I'd likely be dead now, so if nothing else, this allergy has allowed me to hang around long enough for me to make *you*.

Your shoe size will be eleven.

You'll need to start shaving almost on the day you turn sixteen.

You'll get acne – not badly, but badly enough. It'll start at thirteen and, despite conventional wisdom, it never goes away. As far as looks go, you did pretty well there, too, and because of this, for the rest of your life people will do nice things for you for no apparent reason. You'd be a fool to think that everybody gets the same treatment. No way, José. Everybody else in the world has to jump up and down and scream to even get served a cup of coffee. You just have to sit there looking vacant, and they'll be tamping free T-bills into your underwear's stretchy hem. Having said all this, I managed to screw up this once fortunate face. The conventional wisdom is true as regards faces: by mid-adulthood, what's inside you becomes what people see on the outside. Car thieves look like car thieves, cheats look like cheats, and calm, reflective people look calm and reflective. So be careful. My face is like yours, but I ended up turning it into the face of failure. I look bitter. If you saw me walking down the street, you'd think to yourself, "Hey, that guy looks bitter." It's really that simple. My face is now like one of those snow domes you buy in tourist traps. People look into it and wonder, *How badly was he damaged by the massacre? Has he hit bottom yet? I hear he used to be religious, but it's not in his eyes anymore. I wonder what happened?*

Just don't screw your life up the way I did, but you're young, and because you're young, you won't listen to anybody, anyway, so what's the point of advice? This whole letter is a pointless exercise.

Wait – here's a biggie: you're prone to blacking out when you drink. Using something else along with the booze gives you longer blackouts more quickly, and a blacked-out experience can never be retrieved. At least, I have yet to retrieve one, and I've *tried,* thank you. I even went to a hypnotist a few years ago, one I know was a medically trained hypnotist, not some quack, and . . . *nada.*

What else? What else? It's better to eat lots of meals throughout the day instead of just three. Also, if you want to get close to somebody, you have to tell him or her something intimate about yourself. They'll tell you something intimate in return, and if you keep this going, maybe you'll end up in love.

You probably won't be very talkative, but your mind ought to be pretty alive most of the time. Find a puppet and make it do the talking for you.

Finally: You will be able to sing. You will have a lovely voice. Find something valuable to sing, and go out and sing it. It's what I ought to have done.

The hospital just phoned. My father slipped on his kitchen floor and cracked some ribs and possibly did some cardiac bruising. Could I please go to his place and gather some basic items for him?

"He gave you my phone number? I'm unlisted."

"He did."

"But he's never even phoned me."

"He knew it by heart."

The nurse said she'd leave a list of items and a key in an envelope down by reception. "I have a hunch you two don't get along and he needs a few days without incident. You don't have to see him."

"Right."

Dad's apartment is somewhere in North Vancouver – off Lonsdale, not even that far from Mom's condo. I could simply not go, but I have to admit, I'm tempted.

*   *   *

Dad lives on the eighteenth floor; God must like elevators. The apartment is a generic unit built in maybe 1982, about ten minutes before the entire city went crazy on teal green, a color I'm forced to endure at least a few times a week as a subcontractor. Dad's place is dark yellow with plastic mock-Tiffany lampshades, and brown-and-orange freckled indoor-outdoor carpeting. My job in the renovation business has turned me into a fixtures snob: the hardware-store cupboard door fronts are all stained like burnt coffee; the Dijon-colored walls have remained unmodified since the the rollers were put away in 1982. The windows face the mountains – the apartment receives no direct sunlight except for maybe two minutes at sunset on the longest day of the year. This is not an apartment in which fresh vegetables are consumed. It smells like a dead spice rack.

The August heat brought out the full aroma of the furniture – homely crappy stuff Reg kept, nay, *demanded* to keep, after he and Mom split: a brown plaid recliner aimed at a TV inside an oak console like they used to give away on game shows. On a cheap colonial kitchen table was a box of insurance documents; a half-eaten can of Beef-a-

Roni and a spoon lay on the floor where I guess he fell. Jesus, how depressing.

The bedroom is where the good stuff ought to have been, at least that's what I'd hoped. Again, dark furniture left over from his split-up with Mom, and all of it too big for the room. On his dresser top was a blue runner, on which stood framed photos, yellowed and bleached, of him, Mom, Kent and me. I remember when each photo was taken – the sittings were torture; it was simply weird that he had photos of Mom and me there. Kent sure, but *me*? And *Mom*?

His bed was queen-sized. If he'd had a twin bed, it would have been so bleak I'd have had to flee. I went and sat down on his preferred side, which smelled of pipe tobacco, smoke and dust. There was an olive rotary phone, a can of no-name tonic water and an aspirin bottle. What would be in the two drawers beneath it – girlie mags? A salad bowl filled with condoms? No. He had Bibles, *Reader's Digest* Condensed Books and clipped newspaper articles. Oh, to find something human like an escort service card or a gin bottle to go with the tonic, but no. Just this garage sale jumble, all of it so blank, so totally anti-1999 as to evoke thoughts of time travel back to, say, North Platte, Nebraska, circa 1952. The thought of my silent, sour-faced father walking from room to room – rooms in which phones never ring, where other voices never enter – it almost broke my heart, but then I realized, Wait a second, this is Reg, not some monk. Also, before I take too much pity on him, I ought to note how much his place is like *my* place.

I fetched the items on the list: pajamas, T-shirts, under-wear, socks, and so on. The contents of his dresser were all folded and color-coded as if waiting for inspection by some cosmic drill sergeant on Judgment Day.

I grabbed his bottles of old people's medications, a toothbrush and contact lens gear and headed for the front door where, passing a little side table, I came close to missing a photo of my father with a woman – an ample and cheery woman – in a pink floral dress. His arms were around her shoulders, and, alert the media, there was a *smile* on his face.

The heart of a man is like deep water.

*　　*　　*

I've been writing these last bits in a coffee shop. I'm now officially one of those people you see writing dream diaries and screenplays in every Starbucks, except if you saw me writing, you'd maybe guess I was faking some quickie journal entries to hand my anger management counselor. So be it.

Around three I went to the hospital with the white plastic Save-On shopping bag full of Reg's personal needs. In the building's lobby I had the choice of dumping it at the desk or asking what room my father was in. What came over me? It was nearly eleven years since I'd last spoken with him, me shouting curses while he lay on the blue rug at the old house with his shattered knee. We hadn't spoken at Kent's wedding, the funeral or yesterday's memorial. I figured he must have learned something between then and now.

The hospital's central cooling system was malfunctioning, and guys in uniforms with tool kits were in the elevator with me. When I got off on the sixth floor, I was invisible to the staff, while the air-conditioning guys were treated like saviors.

I found Reg's room. The odor outside it reminded me of

luggage coming onto the airport carousels from China and Taiwan – mothballs, but not quite. I had a short moment of disbelief when I was outside the door and technically only a spit away from *him*. Yes? No? Yes? No? Why not? I went in – a shared room, a snoring young guy with his leg in a cast near the door. On the other side of a flimsy veil lay my father.

"Dad."

"Jason."

He looked awful – bloodless, white and unshaven – but certainly alert. "Here's your stuff . . . the hospital asked me to get it."

"Thank you."

Silence.

He asked, "Did you have trouble finding anything?"

"No. Not at all. Your place is pretty orderly."

"I try and run a tight ship."

I shivered when I thought of his hot dusty lightless hallway, his mummified TV set, his kitchen cupboards laden with tins and packets and boxes of rationlike food, and his cheapskate lifestyle, in which not tipping some poor waitress is viewed more as a way of honoring God than of being a miser with one foot in the grave. I held out the bag. "Here you go."

"Put it on the window ledge."

I did this. "What did the doctor say?"

"Two cracked ribs and bruising like all get-out. Maybe some cardio trauma, which is why they're keeping me here."

"You feel okay?"

"It hurts to breathe."

Silence.

I said, "Well, I ought to go, then."

"No. Don't. Sit on the chair there."

The guy in the other bed was snoring. I wondered what on earth to say after a decade of silence. "It was a nice memorial. Barb sure gets excited."

"Kent should never have married her."

"Barb? Why not?"

"No respect. Not for her elders."

"Meaning *you*."

"Yes, meaning me."

"You actually think you deserve respect after what you said to her?"

He rolled his eyes. "From your perspective – from the way *you* look at the world, no."

"What's that supposed to mean?"

"It means, *relax*. It means Kent ought to have married someone closer to his own heart."

I huffed.

"Don't play dumb with me, Jason. It always looked bad on you. Kent needed a more devoted wife."

I was floored. "Devoted?"

"You're being obtuse. Barb could never fully surrender to Kent. And without surrender, she could never be a true wife."

I fidgeted with his water decanter, which seemed to be made of pink pencil eraser material. Why does everything in a hospital have to be not just ugly, but evocative of quick, premature and painful death? I said, "Barb has a personality."

"I'm not saying she doesn't."

"She's the mother of your two grandchildren."

"I'm not an idiot, Jason."

"How could you have gone and said something so insensitive last night – suggesting that one of the kids might not even have a soul. Are you really as mindlessly cruel as you seem?"

"The modern world creates complex moral issues."

"*Twins* are not complex moral issues. *Twins* are *twins*."

"I read the papers and watch the news, Jason. I see what's going on."

I changed the subject. "How long are you in here?"

"Maybe five days." He coughed, and it evidently hurt. Good.

"Are you sleeping okay?"

"Last night like a baby."

A mood swept over me, and as with any important question in life, the asking felt unreal, like it came from another person's mouth: "How come you accused me of murder, Dad?"

Silence.

"Well?"

Still no reply.

I said, "I didn't come in here planning to ask you this. But now that I have, I'm not leaving until you give me a reply."

He coughed.

"Now don't *you* play the little old man with me. Answer me."

My father turned his face away, so I walked to the head of the bed, squatted down and grabbed his head, forcing him to lock eyes with me. "Hi, Dad. I asked you a question, and I think you owe me an answer. Whaddya say, *huh*?"

His expression wasn't hate and it wasn't love. "I didn't accuse you of murder."

"Really now?"

"I merely pointed out that you had murder in your heart, and that you chose to act on that murderous impulse. Take from that what you will."

"That's all?"

"Your mother, as you'll recall, stopped the dialogue at that point."

"Mom stood up for me."

"You really don't understand, do you?"

"What – there's something to *understand* here?"

My father said, "You were perfect."

"I was *what*?"

"Your soul was perfect. If you'd died in the cafeteria, you'd have gone directly to heaven. But instead you chose murder, and now you'll never be totally sure of where you're headed."

"You honestly believe this?"

"I'll always believe it."

I let go of his head. The guy in the next bed was rousing. My father said, "Jason?" but I was already through the door. From his cracked and bruised chest he yelled the words, "All I ever wanted for you was the Kingdom."

He'd stuck his saber through my gut. He'd done his job.

* * *

It's around midnight. After I left Dad, my choice was to either become very drunk or write this. I chose to write this. It felt kind of now-or-never for me.

Back to the massacre.

Two weeks after the attack, videocassettes were mailed to

the school's principal, to the local TV news programs and to the police. They had been made by the three gunmen using a Beta cam they'd rented from the school's A/V crib. It pretty much laid out what they were going to do, how they were going to do it, and why – the generic sort of alienation we've all become too familiar with during the 1990s.

You'd have thought these tapes would have cleared me completely, but no. *Someone* had to arrange for the tapes to be mailed, and *someone* had to be filming these three losers spouting their crap: it was a hand-held camera. So even when I was cleared, in the public mind I was never spotlessly cleared. There was never any doubt with the police and RCMP, thank God, but let me tell you, once people get a nutty idea in their head, it's there for good. And to this day, whoever shot the video and mailed the dubs remains a mystery.

A few celebrities emerged from the massacre, the first being me, semi-redeemed after two weeks of exhaustive investigation revealed my obvious innocence. But of course, for the only two weeks that really mattered, I was demonized.

The second celebrity – and the biggest – was Cheryl. When she wrote GOD IS NOWHERE/GOD IS NOW HERE, she'd finished with GOD IS NOW HERE, which was taken for a miracle, something I find a bit of a stretch.

The third celebrity was Jeremy Kyriakis, the gun boy who repented and was then vaporized for doing so.

During the weeks I spent in motel rooms, I often had nothing to do except reread the papers and watch TV while I exceeded my daily allotment of sedatives and thought of Cheryl, about our secret life together and – I can't express what it felt like to be trashed for two weeks while at the same time Jeremy Kyriakis was being offered as poster boy for the it's-never-too-late strain of religious thinking. It was Jeremy who took out most of the kids by the snack machines – and shot off Demi Harshawe's foot, too – as well as producing most of the trophy case casualties, but he *repented* and so he was forgiven and lionized.

In the third week after the massacre, Kent returned to Alberta and we moved back into the house. Now I was a semi-hero, but at that point screw *everybody*. On the first Monday, around 9:15 in the morning, just after the soaps had started on TV, Mom asked if I was going to go back to school. I said no, and she said, "I figured so. I'm going to sell the house. It's in my name."

"Good idea."

There was a pause. "We should probably move away for a while. Maybe to my sister's place in New Brunswick. And change your hair like they do on crime shows. Find a job. Try and put time between you and the past few weeks."

I made some forays into the world, but wherever I went I caused a psychic ripple that made me uncomfortable. At the Capilano Mall, one woman began crying and hugging me, and wouldn't let go, and when I finally got her off me, she'd left a phone number in my hand. Downtown I was spotted by a group of these dead Goth girls, who followed me everywhere, touching the sidewalk where my feet had just been as if their palms could receive heat from the act. As for school-related activities like sports, they were off the menu, too. Nobody ever phoned to apologize for abandoning me. The principal showed up on Tuesday – the For Sale sign was already on the lawn by then – and there were still eggs and spray-painted threats and curses all over the house's walls. Mom let him in, asked if he'd like some coffee and settled him at the kitchen table with a cup, and then she and I went through the carport door and drove down to Park Royal to shop for carry-on baggage. When we got back a few hours later he was gone.

A week later I was out in the front yard with a wire brush, dishwashing soap and a hose, trying to scrape away the egg stains; the proteins and oils had soaked into the wood, and scrubbing was turning out to be pointless. A minivan full of charismatic *Youth Alive!* robots pulled into the driveway. There were four of them, led by the intrusive jerk Matt. They were wearing these weird, desexed jeans that somehow only *Alive!*ers seemed to own. They all had suntans, too, and I remembered an old brochure: "Tans come from the sun, and the sun is fun, and *Youth Alive!*, while being a serious organization charged with the care of youth, is also a fun, sunny, lively kind of group, too."

I had nothing to say to these guys, and ignored them as my father might ignore a pickup truck full of satanists listening to rock music being played backward.

Matt said, "Taking it easy, huh? We thought we'd come visit. You're not back in school."

I carried on scrubbing the house with steel wool.

"It's been a rough few weeks for all of us."

I looked at them. "Please leave."

"But, Jason, we just got here."

"Leave."

"Oh, come on, you can't be . . ."

I blasted them with the garden hose. They stood their ground: "You're upset. That's natural," Matt said.

"Do any of you have any idea what traitorous scum you are?"

"Traitors? We were merely helping the RCMP."

"I learned about all of your help, thank you."

In spite of the hose, the foursome advanced. Were they going to kidnap me or group hug me? Lay their bronzed fingers on my head and pronounce me whole and returned to the flock?

Then a shot was fired – and two more – by my mother from the second floor. She was making craters in the lawn with Reg's .410. She blasted out the minivan's lights. "You heard Jason. Leave. Now."

They did, and for whatever reason, the cops never showed up.

Word of Mom and the gun must have kept away quite a few potential visitors. There were a few press people; a few family friends who'd vanished during those first two weeks; some *Alive!* girls leaving baked goods, cards and flowers on the doorstep, all of which I unwrapped and threw into the juniper shrubs for the raccoons. In any event, we never let anybody through our front door; within a month, the house was sold and we'd moved to my aunt's place in Moncton, New Brunswick.

My brain feels sludgy. It's late, but Joyce is always up for a good walk.

*   *   *

Just in the door. A warm, dry night out, my favorite kind of weather, and so rare here. During Joyce's walk I saw a car like the one Cheryl's mother, Linda, used to drive – a LeBaron with wood siding. The model looked good for the first week it was out, but a decade of sun and salt and frost have made it resemble the kind of car people in movies drive after a nuclear war.

Linda wrote me some time after we moved away; the letter is one of the few items I've kept across the years. It was mailed to my old address and forwarded to my aunt's house. It read:

Dear Jason,

I'm deeply ashamed that I've not contacted you before this. In the midst of losing Cheryl, we were vulnerable and chose to listen to strangers and not our own hearts. At the time when you needed comfort and support the most, we turned away from you, and it's something Lloyd, Chris and I face every day in the mirror. I don't ask your forgiveness, but I do request your understanding.

It's been a few months since October 4, but it feels like ten years. I've quit my job and, in theory, I'm supposed to be overseeing the Cheryl Anway Trust, but all I do is wake up, dress myself, drink some coffee and drive down to this office space we've rented on Clyde Avenue. There's not much for me to do here. Cheryl's *Youth Alive!* friends take care of the Trust's every function – handling cash, cheques and credit card receipts, sending thank-you notes, manning the phones, filling out tax forms, and so on. It's a busy place, but I don't fit in. I wish I could derive some sort of consolation from the Trust's success, but I don't, and they all work so hard – they've got bumper stickers, bracelets and postcards, and, for what it's worth, a ghostwriter will soon be doing a book about Cheryl's life which may or may not help other young people or their parents. It won't help me. I shouldn't be telling you this – this letter may never even find you – but nothing in the past months has brought me any solace, and how could it? In the last year of her life, my daughter was no longer my daughter. She was somebody else. I have no idea who it was who died in the shooting. What sort of mother would say that about her child?

I've just had one of those moments. Maybe you've had them, too – a moment when the distance and perspective I think I've put between me and Cheryl's shooting dissolves, and I'm right back on October 4 again – and then suddenly it's months later and I'm a middle-aged woman sitting in a rainy suburb on a weekday, and her daughter is dead for no reason, and she never knew her daughter at all. Her daughter chose something else; Cheryl chose something else over me and what our family offered, and she did it with smiles for everybody, but with condescension. And what am I to do? There is nothing I can do. Some man or woman is going to write Cheryl's life story, and they're going to ask me questions and I won't have a thing to say.

I don't know if I'm angry with Cheryl or angry at the universe. Do you get angry, Jason? Do you? Do you ever just want to take your car out onto the highway and gun the engine as fast as you can and then close your eyes and see what happens?

Lloyd and Chris are taking things much better than I am. I'm lucky in that regard. Chris is young – he'll heal.

There will be scars, but he'll make it through okay. We have no idea what to do with him and school. He's having a hard time readjusting at Delbrook, which they've just reopened – they bulldozed the cafeteria and built a new one in just four weeks. We might have to send him to a private school, which we can't afford. That's for another letter.

Jason, I apologize. You don't need this on top of everything else, but then maybe you *do*. Maybe you need to know that there was someone else out there who loved the girl beneath the perfect smile, the girl who, to my mind, foolishly prayed for suffering so she could play at martyrdom. Jason, there's no one to talk to about this. All systems have failed me. In five minutes I'll be fine again for a while, but right now the inside of my head feels like Niagara Falls without the noise, just this mist and churning and no real sense of where earth ends and heaven begins.

I beg your forgiveness, wherever you are. Please write or phone or visit if you can. Please think of me kindly and know that is how I think of you,

Yours,
Linda Anway

A letter from Mr. Anway came three days later:

Dear Jason,
Linda tells me she has written to you, and in so doing she has shamed me. How can I thank you for your bravery on that horrible morning? You saved the lives of so many children without thought of your own

safety. I drove down to your house earlier today, but it had been sold quite a while ago. There was no forwarding address for you, but I'm hoping Canada Post will track down your family with this letter.

Linda hasn't been herself since October 4. How could she be? I don't know what she wrote in her letter, but please take into account that we've both been running on empty for months now. That I didn't recognize the media's smear job of your fine nature is a stain I will take to the grave.

I asked if she had described the funeral for you, and she hadn't. So I will. It was Tuesday, the eleventh of October, a week after the shooting. I had thought the week would allow things to cool down, but instead things snowballed, and have never stopped snowballing.

We opted to have a graveside ceremony only. This was a tactical decision made by Linda and me. The people from *Youth Alive!* wanted to run the show, with no regard for our wishes. We figured they'd be having events of their own soon enough (we were right) and we wanted something that was entirely ours, and more intimate. This was a mistake.

For traffic and crowd control reasons, the police had asked that we not have a cortège drive to the cemetery, but that we meet the coffin there. We thought they were overreacting, but we went along with their suggestion: another bad idea, as it turned out. By two in the afternoon there were hundreds of cars parked on the sides of the road around the cemetery. The RCMP escorted us in, and the cemetery was overrun with (the papers reported) about two thousand people. My skin crawled. That's a cliché, but now I know what it means – like a slug crawling down the small of your back.

There was a large white-and-blue-striped canvas awning over Cheryl's grave area, and that was good, but what made me furious was that the *Youth Alive!* people had brought hundreds of black felt markers, and passed them out to everybody, and by the time we got there, Cheryl's casket was densely covered both with teenagers, and with the sorts of things teenagers write. They were treating my daughter's casket like a yearbook. Maybe I was mad because I'd chosen the casket in Cheryl's favorite shade of white, slightly pearly, and I'd been so pleased. Linda was upset about the felt-penning, too, but we bowed to the inevitable. I suppose it's cheerful, really, to be buried with the goodwill of your friends all around you. Linda and I were offered pens, but we declined.

Before Cheryl's funeral, Linda, Chris and I had attended two other funerals. I had thought they would prepare us for Cheryl's, but no, there's nothing that prepares you for the funeral of your own child. The minister was Pastor Fields. He did a fine job of the service, if I may say so, even if it was a bit too preachy for my taste.

I'm still unsure what Cheryl found in religion, but I'd always thought her conversion was too extreme, and so did Linda. Linda says you've had a falling out with your religious friends, and even though they work like Trojans on the Cheryl Anway Trust, I'm with you all the way in thinking that they're slightly creepy. And it was a shock how quickly and how powerfully they denounced you. It's because I listened to them, and not my own heart, that I'm sending you a pathetic letter so long after the fact, instead of having invited you over to our home ages ago.

This letter has become difficult to write, and it's through no fault of yours, Jason. You know what it is? I wish I'd taken one of those pens and written something on Cheryl's coffin. Why didn't I? What foolish pride prevented me from doing something so innocent and loving? Just one more thing to take to the grave with me. Sometimes it feels as if everything in life is just something we haul into the grave. Cheryl's *Alive!* friends look forward to the grave the same way Chris and Cheryl used to look forward to Disney World. I can't share in this excitement, probably because I'm about thirty years closer to death than they are. They keep referring to Cheryl and her notebook with GOD IS NOW HERE as some sort of miracle, and this I can't understand. It's like a twelve-year-old girl plucking daisy petals. *He loves me, he loves me not.* It doesn't feel miraculous to me. But the kids down at the Trust office talk about miracles all the time, and this, too, baffles me. They're always asking for miracles, and finding them everywhere. Inasmuch as I am a spiritual man, I do believe in God – I think that He created an order for the world; I believe that, in constantly bombarding Him with requests for miracles, we're also asking that He unravel the fabric of the world. A world of continuous miracles would be a cartoon, not a world.

I wish we'd rented a boat and gone out into the Straits of Juan de Fuca and beached on some island and taken Cheryl into some woods, located a nice meadow, and buried her there among the wild daisies and ferns. Then I would feel she's at some kind of peace. But her grave now? I went up there yesterday and it was a mound of flowers and teddy bears and letters. And in the rain they'd all melted together, and it shouted confusion and rage and anger at me, which is what one ought to feel after such a heinous crime; but graves are for peace, not for rage.

Wherever this letter finds you, I hope it finds you well and at peace, or something like it. When you return to North Van, might I ask you and your family over for dinner? It's the very least we could do.

Yours fondly,

Lloyd Anway

This arrived two days after Mr. Anway's letter:

Jason,

I just caught my dad mailing you a letter. He tried to hide it between some bills, and when I pushed him, he told me that Mom had also written you, which wigged me out completely. I can all too well imagine the crock of lies he fed you. Mom, too. You need to know that everything they tell you, *everything*, is outright crap. From the word go, they've hated you. After it happened, they took all the photos of you in Cheryl's bedroom and scratched out your face. There would be whole evenings when Cheryl's hypocritical preacher pals would sit in our living room and totally trash you with Mom and Dad. They reduced you to a scab lying on a floor beneath a toilet being carried away by beetles bit by bit. Man, they were *brutal*, and they were extra brutal when they talked about, or rather talked *around*, sex. I mean, let's face it, the two of you were an item, but the *Alive!*oids made it sound like rape, and that it was your sole job in life to corrupt Cheryl. And once they'd tied the noose for you, they'd lay into how you always seemed like the kind of guy who'd plan, and assist in murdering a whole school just to kill the girl he'd worked so hard to corrupt. I mean, get *real*. Some nights I had to leave the house. Most nights, actually.

Mitchell Van Waters, Jeremy Kyriakis and Duncan Boyle were in my grade, and they were such total wipeouts that people could barely remember they existed. They'd come into English class in these beat-up black leather jackets, acting like they were big-shot political guys starting a revolution, and they'd sit there writing lyrics from Skinny Puppy on their cargo pants with felt pens and Liquid Paper. I remember watching Mitchell and Duncan having a wicked scrap with hunting knives down by the portables, all because Duncan brought a six-sided dice, not a twelve-sided dice, for one of those role-playing games they were into. In social studies, Duncan brought in a solid-state panel from a TV set and spent the class in the last row writing hex symbols all over it, but they were fake symbols he was inventing, which looked a lot like the pictures of crop circles he'd photocopied for class the year before. And they wondered why nobody paid them any attention? They were messes, and there was no way you and they even breathed from the same atmosphere. So when they said you were connected to them? I think not.

I was thinking about you and October 4. You've seen the TV stuff like everyone else, but you left the scene and I don't think you ever came back, and maybe you don't know what it was like to have been there.

I was in PE, and during the class jog up the mountain, my friend Mike and I cut out and went down Queens Avenue to smoke. It was a beautiful day. Why waste it with a bunch of jocks? We got to talking with these three girls from the grade below us who were headed to the Safeway deli down at Westview. Then we heard some shots. Funny, I'd never heard a real gun fired in my life, but I knew exactly what it was. So did Mike. We heard a siren, some more shots and – I bet you didn't know this, but that first siren wasn't for massacre victims, it was for that guy you hammered down by the shop classes. Anyway, the five of us decided to walk up the hill, and the shots continued and then the SWAT team, the Navy SEALS, James Bond, and, I don't know, Charlie's Angels, all arrived at once. And all of the students pouring out of the school? Their heads looked like Sugar Crisp being poured from a box. Everybody was running as fast as they could, but they were all trying to look back, too, and so they were wiping out all over. By the time we neared the front of the school, they were hauling out bodies and, well, no need to go into that. We were moved up to the top of the hill, but we could tell exactly who had blood on them and who was being treated. I saw you, and you were covered in blood, but you were walking, so I assumed you were okay. And then I suddenly had a chill and I knew Cheryl was dead. I think ESP is BS, but that's what I felt.

The rest of the day was a war zone. All of the parents began showing up from work and home, and they'd leave their cars parked wherever with the engines still running and the doors open. Once family members hooked up, the RCMP moved them up and onto the football field, and so the parking lot became the place for an ever-shrinking number of parents without children. Mom and Dad showed up, and around 3:30 we heard the news about Cheryl. Our brains were so fried by that point that it didn't even make sense. Mrs. Wong from next door drove us to the hospital in Dad's car. There was no way he could drive. Her two kids were in the caf but were unhurt. She'd have driven us to Antarctica if we'd asked.

The hospital was another scene altogether – dead and mended bodies rolling around like shopping carts in a supermarket. I don't even know why they or we stuck around. It was kind of pointless by then. I mean, we knew Cheryl was lost even before we arrived. We were so messed up.

When it turned dark out, I was still in my gym clothes from PE class. Somebody, I don't remember who, gave me a windbreaker, and it was as I was zipping it up that I heard the first rumor about YOU, there in the hospital lobby. The rumors didn't even start small. Right from the outset YOU were the mastermind, and when Mom and Dad found out, Mom went hysterical, and they had to give her a barbiturate, which is like this elephant pill from the 1950s. Dad took something, too, and for the first week they were floating on these things. Mom still is. I can always tell when it's time for her next dose, because her breathing goes all choppy. They really were out of their minds that you were to blame. I tried sticking up for you, and nearly got excommunicated from the family. And what did you ever do to those *Alive!*oids? They were brutal about you.

But I was going to say that when it was announced at the end of the second week that you were innocent of all charges, Mom went even crazier, and dragged Dad down with her. They refused to believe the RCMP's report. The you-know-whos had done a real number on the two of them.

Anyway, this is the longest letter I've ever written, and the most focused I've been since October 4. You've moved or split town or something – good for you. Lucky you. Can I come escape to wherever you are?

Be strong, buddy,

Chris

Through a Starbucks window I'm watching a sunset the color of children's aspirin as I crash-land on two clonaze-pams. I paid twenty bucks a pop for them from some Persian brat in his daddy's BMW, down at the corner of Fourth and Lonsdale – just blocks away from Mom's place.

God. Now I *do* feel like I'm prepping for an anger

management class. But there's no class, and if you're still doing what I'm doing at my age, then a class isn't what you need. Money, maybe? Kent got drunk as a log at his wedding, and while I was dancing with a bridesmaid, and he with Barb, he looped past me, stuck his face into mine, and with a hot breath of champagne, chicken breast and vegetable medley said, "You'll never be rich because you don't like rich people." And then he whirled off. And he was right: I don't like rich people, with their built-in towel racks that need a heating system that comes from Scotland – *Scotland!* – with their double-door refrigerators with non-magnetic surfaces to discourage the use of fridge magnets, and with their Queen Charlotte Islands red cedar shoe closets that smell like saunas.

Here's what I did wrong: I installed the built-in towel racks on the wrong side of the bath, and Les went mental on me because the owner won't surrender the weekly payment until it's done properly. I care but I don't care, but then Les is furious with the universe because his kid has a cataract, so I *do* care, but then at the same time, for God's sake, it's just a *towel rack* for some guy who, for whatever reason, needs to get his jollies with a warm towel every morning. So in the end, it's not possible to care – it's just towels. If Rich Guy uses one towel a day for a decade, it's still going to cost him over eighty cents a towel.

$$\frac{\$3,000.00}{365 \times 10} = 82¢$$

And in any event, best friends don't fistfight over towels or towel racks – or, if I ruled the world, they wouldn't.

Forget about ruling the world, I can barely get the automatic doors at Save-On-Foods to acknowledge my existence. So I have to take what life sends me. I put a smile on it. I seethe. I leave work a few hours early. I get cranked in a downtown parking lot. I fly high and develop elaborate schemes to elevate human consciousness. I come down. I get cranked again, but I suspect the new amphetamine is cut with milk sugar, so I enjoy it less the second time. I think, *Wow, have I really watched two sunrises and two sunsets without having slept?* I come down hard. I buy clonazepams from Persian twerps. I sit in a café and scribble on pink invoice papers.

Off to Mom's. Got to rescue Joyce.

*   *   *

It's the next morning, or at least McDonald's hasn't switched over to their lunch menu yet. A fast-food breakfast; drops of grease have elevated this morning's pink invoice paper into a stained-glass document.

My brain feels like a cool, deep lake. Did I really sleep for twelve hours? I'll even make it to work by noon today, which will probably put Les in such a good mood that he'll forget the string of six near-satanic messages he dumped into my answering machine.

Well, nephews, when I went to my mother's place last night after Starbucks, your mother, Barb, was there, leaning on the kitchen counter, and the big discussion was about why Reg is such a bastard, a subject my mother has given much thought to.

As I walked in the door, they both took one look at me, and Mom said, "*You* – into the shower right now. When you're finished, change into something from the guest room closet. I've got some cream of cauliflower soup and French bread here. You'll eat some of that, and *then* you're going right to bed in the guest room. Got it?"

From the bathroom, I heard some of what my mother and your mother were saying.

"Well, you know, the initial attraction was that his family grew daffodils – still grows them. I thought that was so amazing – I thought only good people could grow daffodils."

"What would bad people grow?"

"I don't know. Bats? Mushrooms? Algae? But daffodils – they're the most innocent flower on earth. They're a member of the onion family. Did you know that?"

"I didn't."

"Learn something new every day."

"Aren't narcissus the same as daffodils?"

"They are. Most people think they're different. But they're not."

"Wouldn't a narcissus be, well, not quite evil, but not innocent, either – vain?"

"Reg had an answer for that. Do you want to hear it?"

"Tell me."

"He said, 'Who are we to slap the human sin of vanity onto some poor flower that did nothing more than be given a name?'"

"That's kind of nice."

"He also looked at the flowers at our wedding – anthuriums, ginger and birds-of-paradise – he said afterward that he thought they were 'slutty.'"

"Oh."

The two women watched me enter the kitchen. Neither of them had any illusions. Mom said, "Here's some orange juice. Your system's probably screaming for vitamin C."

"Jesus, Jason. Shave already. You could sharpen a hunting knife on your five o'clock shadow." Mom placed a soup bowl onto the counter. To them it was nothing, but to me this moment was a brief taste of heaven.

Barb asked my mom, "When did Reg start turning gonzo on you?"

"With religion?"

"Yeah."

"Maybe a year after Kent was born. There was no specific trigger. Jason, honey, use a napkin, I just washed the floor."

"Overnight?"

"No. I remember his face hardening about the same time – his cheek muscles losing slackness. It was probably something to do with serotonin. If I'd secretly dosed his coffee with Wellbutrin or another one of these new drugs, we'd still be a functioning happy couple. But instead he just kept losing it and losing it. By the time the kids started school, we were in separate beds. I was drinking big time by then. He liked it because it kept me in one place, and because when I was drunk, he didn't need to speak to me. Not like I wanted to speak with him."

*　　*　　*

Cell phone just rang. I have to go. Les says this week's check cleared, so why don't we go have a beer to celebrate? It's 11:00 A.M.

*　　*　　*

Okay, it's been six days since my last entry in this journal, and I'm going to record what happened as fully as I can remember.

Les and I went for a beer at the Lynwood Inn, a blue-collar place down at the docks beneath the Second Narrows Bridge pilings. I don't know if it was the heat, or that we weren't eating the free chicken wings, but by one o'clock we were blotto, when in walked this wharf rat, Jerry, who I met in court in 1992 – he'd been pulled over in an Isuzu pickup loaded with stolen skis. When the next pitcher of beer arrived, Jerry paid from a big roll of bills. He then said he had a seventeen-foot aluminum boat with an Evinrude 50 for sale. It was down on the water and did we want to go for a ride?

The boat was a real sweetheart and dead simple: a hull, an engine, a front windshield and a steering wheel – basically a Honda Civic afloat on the harbor's brilliant glassy water . . . salt mist and galvanized metal; propeller blades churning in jade green water cut with pale blue smoke.

The harbor was dense with freighters, and there was this one Chinese hulk in the midst of loading up on hemlock two-by-fours. Some guy up on deck threw something at us – a lunch bag or something minor, but Jerry drove up to the side of the freighter, which resembled a rusting, windowless ten-story building, and started screaming in Chinese.

"Jerry – where'd you learn Chinese?"

"My ex. Eleven years of my life, and all I'm left with is Cantonese, hep C and advanced skills in seafood cooking." The guy up above disappeared for a second, and Les and I said, "Jerry, let's get out of here," but Jerry wouldn't listen. The guy up above reappeared over the edge and dropped what seemed to be a cast-iron loaf of bread – I have no idea what it was, but it rammed a hole the size of a dinner plate in our boat's hull. We sank quickly, and we swam to land near the Saskatchewan Wheat Pool. We found some ancient rusting rungs, which we climbed up; they put us in a hot, dusty railyard. We'd gotten coated with diesel oil during the swim, and the powdery gray dirt stuck to us like flour on cod. Les was furious because his wife had been haranguing him for years over his taste in clothes, and today was the first day he was wearing a pair of pants she'd bought for him. Les became morose: "She's going to fry my butt."

I said, "Jesus, Jerry, what did you say to that Chinese guy, anyway?"

"Well, he called me some names, and I called him some names, and then he said he'd sink the boat if I kept dissing him, and then he sank the boat. The damn thing was hot as a stove, anyway. Probably better that it sank." Jerry then flipped open his cell phone, saying, "Someone'll come pick us up."

In order to reach the road, we had to cut across eight tracks on which train cars were shunting according to laws unknown to us, each car capable of shredding us into french fries at any moment.

Out at the road, sure enough, there sat a black stretch limo. Its driver was Yorgo, a Russian gorilla who was also a clean freak. He insisted we take off our clothes and put them on a tarp in the trunk. I asked Jerry why there'd be a tarp in the trunk, and he said, "Don't ask."

So we sat in our underwear in the back of this limo. Les discovered some rotgut scotch in the limo's plastic decanter and tanked himself up even further, while Jerry began obsessing about finding identical trousers so Les wouldn't get in trouble with his wife. This struck me as manic, but then the Russian gorilla threw Jerry a Ziploc bag of coke, and I saw where the mania came from.

"I can't do coke. I really can't. Allergies. Anything that ends with '–aine'."

"I've heard of that. More for me, then." Jerry made a noise to Yorgo, and some pills appeared from up front.

"What are they?"

"Well," Jerry said, "one pill makes you bigger, and one pill makes you small."

I took two, and we drove around the city, and reached the conclusion that we needed to buy clothing, but first we had to wash. We bought a squeeze bottle of dish detergent and drove to Wreck Beach, at the base of the cliffs at UBC. Amid the overall nudity, our underwear attracted no notice. We left Les passed out in the car.

Out in the water we used the dish soap to scrape the diesel fuel from our skin, but a group of hippie kids saw us and began screaming at us for using squeeze bottle soap at the beach, and began pelting us with oyster shells, so we dropped the bottle and swam down the shore. Once on land, Jerry stole two towels from a log and we climbed back up the cliff, at which point I remember wanting some of the scotch Les was drinking – and then my blackout. Jerry's magic pills.

*   *   *

The next thing I remember is being in Seattle. Judging by beard stubble it was maybe two nights later. I was on Interstate 5 entering downtown, riding shotgun in an Audi sedan. At the wheel was a skinny junkie-looking guy with chattering teeth. He looked at me and said, "It's okay. You've got the money with you. The important thing to remember is not to panic."

Not to panic? Am I supposed to be not panicking about

something? This wasn't a situation I wanted to be a part of. The car pulled up to a stoplight. I got out and walked through the first door I saw, which happened to be the west lobby entrance of a Four Seasons hotel. I caught sight of myself in a jewelry shop's display case: I was sunburnt and wearing a designer outfit like the ones in magazine spreads that no guy ever wears in real life. I had to shed this ridiculous outfit, but how? Where?

In the vest pocket a palm-thick wad of fifties, but no ID, which might prove to be a problem, what with being a Canadian in the U.S. most likely on shady business. One of Jerry's pills was tucked into a deep corner, so I wiggled it loose and popped it in my mouth. At the bar I ordered a martini and flirted with two women who were up from the Bay Area and who worked for Oracle's PR department. I wasn't in their league, but they were fun, and they made cracks about my jacket. In the men's room I removed it and buried it in the hand towel basket beneath a pile of towels. And then I blacked out once again.

When I came to, I was walking past alders and birches beside a stony mountain river. The river wasn't huge like the Fraser, and it wasn't tiny; it was a mountain river that fed into something larger. It was late afternoon and my hands were behind my head. I could hear someone's feet on the rocks behind me. I looked down and remembered being a kid and staring at sand in the Capilano, seeing flecks of mica and being convinced it was gold.

The river looked cold, and was filled with rocks like the one I'd used to kill Mitchell. And the landscape surrounding the river reminded me of the valley forest by the Klaasen family daffodil farm in Agassiz: the creepy sunless forests carpeted with moss that swallows your feet, and mud that sucks up all noise – summerproof and free of birds.

I turned around to look. Yorgo was behind me, and he cracked me between the shoulders with the barrel of a shotgun. It was just the two of us, and we were clearly on a death march. The tarp in the limo's trunk sprang to mind.

I also noted how quickly my childhood muscle memory for walking atop river rock had returned. Yorgo, I could hear, was having some trouble. He probably grew up in a city.

I didn't want to trudge meekly to my fate. To this end I veered ever so slightly toward the wetter, more slippery rocks. It was a simple idea that yielded instant results – I heard Yorgo slip, and as I heard this, I swiveled around and watched him go down hard on the riverbed, his left shinbone snapping like kindling, his weapon clattering off into the water, carried away almost instantly.

I lunged for a river rock and then – time folded over in a Moebius strip – I was once again in the school cafeteria, and there was Mitchell's head, but it was now Yorgo's head, and in my hand was a rock and – suddenly I had the option of murdering again.

*   *   *

I remember after the massacre I heard that people were praying for the killers, and that made me furious. *It's a bit too late to pray for them now, wouldn't you think?* I was livid for years afterward. Why did those prayers bug me so much – people praying for assassins? I began to wonder if it was because I had so much hate in my own heart; it's a truism that the people we dislike the most in this life are the people who remind us of ourselves. I'd gone through my life with this massive chunk of hate inside me like a block of demolished concrete, complete with rusted and twisted metal radiating from the inside. Perhaps I didn't feel I deserved any prayers. For over a decade in my head it's been *Rot in hell, you evil little freaks. No pain is big enough for you, and I wish you were alive so I could blow you up and turn you into a big pile of guts that I could trample all over and douse with gasoline and set on fire.*

I never could see how anything good could come from the Delbrook Massacre. Whenever I've heard people saying, "Look how it's brought us all together," I've had to leave the room or switch the channel. What a feeble and pathetic moral. Just look at our world, so migratory – cars and airplanes and jobs here and there: what does it matter if a few of us who happened to be in this one spot at one moment briefly rallied together and held hands and wore ribbons? Next year, half of us will have moved away, and then where's your moral?

After another few years I simply became tired. I kept on asking for a sign and none ever came – and then there I was on a riverbank with Yorgo, holding a river rock above my head.

*   *   *

I dropped the rock onto a nearby boulder. It sent sparks of granite chips into the air and then quickly huddled lost among thousands of similar rocks. I felt like I had committed an antimurder, like I'd created life where none had existed before.

Yorgo said, "You're just weak. You're too frightened to kill me."

I looked at him, his tibia poking into the drape of his slacks. "That may be the case, Yorgo, but it doesn't look to me like you're going anywhere soon. And *what* – you despise me for not killing you?"

He sneered my way.

"You do, don't you?"

Yorgo spat to his left.

I said, "What a loser. Give me your cell phone."

His hand went to his coat pocket. He removed it, and just as I was about to take it, he tossed it sideways toward the river.

I asked him, "Where are we?"

He looked away.

"I see. You're going to be cute with me. That makes a lot of sense." I looked at the rocks around us. "You know, Yorgo, the easiest thing for me to do would be to build a cairn of river rocks on top of you. It'd take me thirty minutes to do, and it would quite easily keep you in place until this winter's flooding sweeps away both it and your remains."

I could tell Yorgo was catching my drift. I walked up to the riverbank and saw no evidence of roads, paths or people. This was good, in that it decreased the chance of having been seen by a jogger or fisherman. I listened for cars or a highway – none. I came back to him. "I'm not going to do anything, Yorgo. Not for now. I'm going to walk away from here, and when I find a phone I will call one person for you and tell them where you are and that your leg is wrecked."

Yorgo remained quiet.

"Or I can simply leave. So if you want to have even a sliver of hope, you'd best give me a number to call."

I walked away.

"Stop!" Yorgo yelled out a phone number. I found a pen in my pants pocket and wrote it on the flesh at the base of my thumb.

I walked west. As the light entered its final waning, I came upon a field with a few cattle, so I hopped the barbed wire, trudged across the field and made my way on a paved road out toward a highway that glowed in the distance, maybe an hour's walk away. The nighttime summer haze was soaking up the highway's car headlights and street lamps, and it was shooting that light skyward, as brightly as the Las Vegas Strip ever did. The farm buildings were built in the Canadian style; I figured the highway had to be the Trans-Canada, and to judge by the mountains faintly contoured against the night sky, I was still in the Fraser Valley, most likely not too far from the Klaasen family farm.

Like most suburbanites, I'm creeped out by agricultural areas. Every footstep reverberated clearly and I began imagining I was hearing someone *else's* footsteps. I looked at the darkened fields and unlit sheds and junked cars. The air smelled of manure, and I wondered if I'd see methane will-o'-the-wisps dancing beyond the road. I remembered Grandma Klaasen hectoring Grandpa about devil worshipers stealing their rototiller, about their vanishing pets and about bodies that were always being found in the lakes and streams and ditches of Agassiz. Crimes are never solved in places like this, only discovered. I imagined headlines in the local shopper papers: MAN'S REMAINS WASH UP IN FRASER RIVER DELTA; GIRL GUIDES FIND SKELETON; RUSSIAN MOTHER ASKS LOCALS FOR HELP LOCATING ONLY SON.

My mind raced with thoughts of death. *Not only am I*

*going to die sooner rather than later, I am going to die alone
and lonely.* But then I remembered, so were my father and
mother. Considering this further, I realized most people I
knew were going to die alone and lonely. Was this life in
general, or was it just me? Did I unwittingly send out the sort
of signals that attract desperate souls? I looked at the
shadows of sleeping cattle and thought, *Lucky farm animals.* Lucky space aliens. Lucky anything-but-humans,
never having to deal with knowing how foul or desperate
their own species is.

I remember once at dinner when I was a kid, I sarcastically
asked Reg what we'd do if we learned to speak with
dolphins. Would we try to convert them? Oddly, he missed
my intent. "Dolphins? Dolphins with the whole English
language at their command?"

"Sure, Dad. Why not?"

"What a good question."

I was so surprised that he'd taken me seriously, that I
became serious in turn. I added, "And we wouldn't even
need translators. We could speak with them just as we're
speaking with each other here."

Reg pulled himself back into his seat, a posture he usually
reserved for deciding which form of punishment we deserved. He said, "In the end, no, there would be no point
converting dolphins, because they never left God's hand. If
anything, we might be asking them what it's like to never
have left, to still be back in the Garden."

Jesus, Dad do you have to be so random? Why is your
kindness or wrath about as predictable as knowing when the
phone is going to ring? I've never known what will set you
off. I still don't. Nobody does. You've built this thing around

you, this place you call the world, but it's not the world – it's Reg's little private club. You're only concerned with making people conform to your own picture of God, never trying to cool the suffering of anyone in pain.

As I walked I tried to recall any crimes or events leading to my riverside drama. I came up blank. How odd to be guilty of enormous acts yet be unaware of them. Maybe *this* is what it feels like to be born with original sin, or rather, to fully *believe* in original sin – to live always with a black sun hovering above you.

And then . . . and then I felt truly old for the first time – old in the sense that I was beyond the point of ever doing something radical or bold to change the course of my life. I was going to remain a contractor's flunky to the grave. I just wanted to put a rusty thick steel Chinese freighter of a wall between me and everyone else's problems. I was sick of wanting money. I was sick of being without a goal.

But I hadn't killed Yorgo.

I stopped and processed this thought. I could have killed him, but I didn't.

Huh.

I was happy, but I was also annoyed. Maybe in spite of all my attempts to block it, my father's sense of will had become my own. Oh, dear God.

The stars above looked milky, like they only do in summer. I saw some sheet lightning off somewhere in the mountains. And then I felt the chunk of concrete hate fall from my chest. A part of my life was over, I realized. I was now in some new hate-free part, and I began to hear the highway's pale drone. To the east was an overpass with a gas station.

Once there I checked to find that I had on me about two hundred bucks Canadian, in twenties that all shared the same serial number. I got change for one and looked at the Pirelli calendar behind the box of Slim Jims; it told me that I'd had that first beer with Jerry five and a half days ago. I phoned in to collect my messages – eleven; as I retrieved them, each push on the pay phone's keypad was like waiting for a punch to the gut. I braced myself for anything.

The first message was from Barb, in tears and without much to say but that she was missing Kent. Following this were calls from my mother, in varying states of sobriety and asking about Joyce's diet, which was her way of saying she was running out of money.

The next was from Kim, asking if I knew where Les was.

Next was Les saying, "Buddy, I owe you big time on this one. I wouldn't donate a kidney for you, but something pretty close. Take tomorrow off, and I still can't believe you let that cute little sales chick sell you that clown suit. Man, she brings you those little cappuccinos with a sprinkle of cinnamon, they play a song you like on the sound system, and before you know it you're looking like a balloon twister at my kid's birthday party."

The next message was from Reg, still at the hospital. "Jason, don't hang up. It's your father, yes, your father. They found something inside me that's not quite right, so they've been holding me here longer. Thank you for bringing in my things. I know you didn't have to do it. I've been considering your reaction to my words. No, I don't think one of Kent's twins is a monster. But then what *does* happen when the self splits? What happens when a cell splits five times, with quintuplets? Each has a unique soul. And what if they made a thousand clones of Frank Sinatra? Each would have a unique soul. So then by extension, Jason, let's say we were to clone an infinite number of souls from one starter soul – yours or mine or the Queen's; whoever's – and say we filled up the universe with this infinite number of cloned souls. Wouldn't this mean that each human soul is infinite as well as full of unimaginable mystery? I leave it at that, son. I've never wanted anything more for you than the Kingdom. Good-bye."

Bastard.

The gas station clerk stared at me. I said, "Bad day," and he said, "Taxi."

"Huh?"

"Your taxi's here."

I'd ordered one. "Tell him to wait a second."

I phoned the number Yorgo'd given me. It rang maybe seven times, and I almost hung up. Then a man answered, some Freon-blooded goon – a crooked cop? A junkie?

"Yorgo wants me to let you know where he is."

"Does he, now?"

"He's stuck up some river. A few miles east of Chilliwack, and I have the feeling he's been there a few times before. Anyway, his left leg's broken. He can't move."

"And this is the number he gave you?"

"Look, I didn't have to tell you this. I'm doing you a favor."

"Yorgo? He's no favor to me."

I asked, "So are you going to go get him?"

"No."

"You're serious."

"Yes, I'm serious. Call the Girl Guides. I have to go now."

He was serious. I hung up. I bought a map and some gum, then taxied back to the Lynnwood Inn to retrieve my truck. Once we arrived, I located my secret key, stashed beneath the fender, and opened the door. I told the cabbie my money was fake, and to pay for the ride I gave him my CD collection. My final request was that he take the map on which I'd written a reasonably detailed description of where Yorgo was and of his condition, and deliver it to the Lonsdale RCMP station. He was to have no idea who left it in the cab. He was a nice guy. He went.

And so I drove back home, where I am now, tired and hungry and coming down off God knows what, and utterly in need of solace.

I guess the thing about blacking out is that you *blacked out*. There's no retrieval. There's not even hunches, and you might as well have been under a general anesthetic. I mean, who was that guy who picked up the phone when I called about Yorgo? I checked the criss-cross phone directory, but it's unlisted. And Jesus, *Yorgo*, out on the rocks, maybe being rescued in an hour or two, either my friend or my enemy for life.

My apartment feels like a mousetrap, not a place to call home. In the bathroom I expected Yorgo's twin brother to jump out from behind the shower curtain with either a silenced Luger or a bottle of vodka to celebrate all that's good in life. When I came out, some beer bottles settled on the balcony, and the clinking made me spasm out of my chair.

I'm going to crash on a friend's couch for the night.

*   *   *

I'm in a Denny's in North Van, Booth Number 7, a dead breakfast in front of me, and a couple arguing about child custody behind me. I've run out of pink invoice paper, so three-ring binder paper from the Staples across the street will suffice.

I slept maybe two hours at my friend Nigel's – he's good at wiring and plastering drywall. He left early to frame a house in West Van, so I had his place to myself. It's a variation of my place: bachelor crap – moldy dishes in the sink; skis leaning against the wall beside the door; newspaper entertainment sections folded open to the TV listings sprayed all over the carpet, which smells like a dog and he doesn't even have a dog.

Here in Denny's Booth Number 7, I can take as much time as I want because the breakfast rush is over, and lunch won't start for maybe an hour. The arguing couple had one final squawk and then left. I've asked the waitress to keep bringing me water so I can flush everything poisonous from my body, the residual alcohol and the residual pills that made me bigger and smaller.

Already I've reconciled myself to the possibility that my truck will explode next time I turn the key, or that they'll find me on the sidewalk outside the Chevron with a pea-sized hole in my third eye. That would be so great, to have it be fast like that.

But there's this other part of me, the part that's shed the block of hate, the part that decided not to kill Yorgo – the part that wants to go further in life. I have to let it be known that I existed. I was real. I had a name. I know there must have been a point to my being here; there *must* have been a point.

Everyone I meet eventually says, "Jason, you saved so many lives back in 1988." Yeah sure, but it wrecked my family, and there are still more people than not who believe I'm implicated in the massacre. Last year I was in the library researching blackouts, and somebody hissed at me – I'm not supposed to notice these things? Cheryl fluked into martyr-dom, and Jeremy Kyriakis scammed his way onto Santa's list of redeemed little girls and boys, but me? Redemption exists, but only for others. I believe, and yet I lack faith. I tried building a private world free of hypocrisy, but all I ended up with was a sour little bubble as insular and exclusive as my father's.

I can feel the little black sun's rays zeroing in on me – burning, burning, burning, like a magnifying glass burning an ant . . . At the count of three, Jason Klaasen, tell the people who you *were* . . . What do you want your clone to know about you?

Dear Clone,
My favorite song was "Suzanne," by Leonard Cohen. I was a courteous driver and I took good care of Joyce. I loved my mama. My favorite color was cornflower blue. If I walked past a shop window and saw a vase or something that was cornflower blue, I would be hyp-notized and would stand there for minutes, just feeling the blueness pump into my eyes. What else? What *else*? I laughed a lot. I never once drove drunk, or even slightly drunk. I'm proud of that. I don't know about the blackouts, but when I was conscious, never.

But, okay, mostly I've been here on Earth for nearly thirty years, and I don't think there is even one person who ever really *knew* me, which is a private disgrace. Cheryl didn't know me properly as an adult, but at least she assumed there was a soul inside my body that merited being known.

Okay then, my nephews, it's lunchtime and this little auto-biography is nearly over except . . . except there's just this one other not-so-little thing remaining to be said, but I'm going to have to mull exactly how I tell you about it. I'm going to go pick up Joyce and head to the beach, and maybe by then my burning brain will have cooled down and I can finally say what I've been avoiding all along.

*   *   *

I'm at the beach, on the same log as before, and I may as well hop right to it.

Just over a year ago, when your mother phoned me to tell me Kent was dead, I drove to her house down in Horseshoe Bay. To get there I had to pass the scene of the accident; highway traffic was closed down to a single lane, and there were shards of glass, strips of chrome, fragments of black plastic fenders and pools of oil on the road. A tow truck was just then hauling the remains of Kent's Taurus onto a flatbed. It was crumpled like picnic trash, and its beige vinyl seats were thick with broken glass. It was a hot afternoon.

I stopped and spoke with a cop at the scene who knew me, and he gave me technical details of the crash – quick and painless. This information still gives me comfort. I suppose that if I hadn't seen the wreck, Kent's death would have been far harder to deal with. But when you see that big chunk of chewed-up scrap metal, the truth is the truth, and the shock passes more quickly.

There was also the pressing need to go down to Barb's – your mother's – house right away. My cell phone's battery had died and there'd been no way to contact my own mother or anybody else. As well, the traffic line-ups for the ferries to Vancouver Island and up the coast were huge and clogging the roads, and I took the wrong exit and ended up being detoured for a few frustrating miles, my temples booming like kettle drums.

When I got to your house, your mother was at the front door talking with the cops. Her eyes were red and wet, and I could tell the police didn't feel good having to leave her like this. When they saw me, they hit the road.

I held Barb tight, and then asked her who in the family she'd called.

She gave me a look that I wasn't expecting – not exactly guilty, and somehow conspiratorial. "Nobody. Did *you*?"

"No. My battery died."

"Jesus, thank God."

"Barb, what are you talking about – you didn't call anyone?"

"No. Just you."

I was confused. I headed for the phone inside. "I'm going to call my mother."

Barb lunged at me and wrested the cordless from my hand. She slammed it down. This was strange, but then people react to grief in so many ways. "We're not phoning anybody. Not yet."

"Barb, we have to call people. Kent's mother. Your mother, for God's sake. It's crazy. We can't *not* phone them. Think about it."

"Jason, there's something you have to help me with first."

"Of course. What can I do?"

137

"Jason, I need to have a baby, and I have to get pregnant right now."

"You have to *what*?"

"You heard me."

"Have a baby."

"Don't be so stupid. Yes."

"Barb, make some sense, okay?"

"Sit down." She motioned to the living room. "Sit on the couch." She grabbed a bottle of Glenfiddich, my Christmas present to Kent, from the sideboard. She poured two glasses and offered me one. "Drink it."

We drank. "I need to have a kid, Jason, and I need to start right now."

"Are you asking me what I think you're asking?"

"Don't be so clueless. Yes, I am. Kent and I have been trying for years, but he shoots blanks mostly. I'm at the peak of my cycle right now, and I have a one-day window to conceive."

"Barb, I don't think – "

"Shut up. Just shut *up*, okay? Genetically, you and Kent are pretty much the same thing. A child by you will look just like a child by Kent. In nine months I want a kid. And I want this kid to look like Kent, and there's only one way that is going to happen."

"Barb, look, I know you're screwed up by – "

"Dammit, shut up, Jason. This is my one chance. It's not like I can do this again in twenty-eight days. I'm not having a baby ten months after Kent's dead. Do some math. Kent was all I had, and unless I do this, there's no way I'll be connected to him. As long as I live. I can't go through life knowing that I at least had this one chance to get it right, even if it means humiliating myself in front of you right now. Like this."

There was a kind of logic to what Barb was saying. The request didn't feel cheap or sleazy. It felt like – and this sounds so bad – the one way to honor my brother. Barb saw this in my eyes. "You'll do it. I can tell. You will."

And this is where I surprised myself. Without fully understanding the impulse, I said, "Okay. I will. But only if we're married."

"What?"

"You heard me. We have to be married."

"You're kidding."

"No. I'm not."

Barb looked at me as if I were a mugger about to swipe her purse. And then her face relaxed. She closed her eyes, made a counting-to-ten face, then opened her eyes and looked at me. "We can't get married right now. City hall is closed."

"We'll go to Las Vegas. We can get married in a chapel on the Strip."

Barb stared at me. "Did you take every cocktail waitress on this side of the harbor to Las Vegas, too?"

I'm stubborn. "Those are my terms. Take them or leave them. We get married first."

"You're nuts."

"No, I'm not nuts. I simply know what I want."

She looked at me. "But I'm already married."

"No you're not. You're a widow."

Barb looked at me for a good half minute. "Okay. Fair enough. Let's drive to the airport."

"Are you – "

"Jason, shut up. Let's drive to the airport now. We'll

catch a nonstop or hub through Los Angeles, and that'll be it."

Within five minutes we were back on the highway, passing the final crash cleanup occurring on the other side of the median. Barb was in tears and asked me not to slow down. I thought this was cold, but she said, "Jason, I will have to drive past there at least four times a day the rest of my life. There's plenty of time for me to look then."

I said, "We don't have any luggage."

"We don't need it. We're going to Las Vegas to get married while the mood seizes us. Ha ha ha."

"You think they'll believe that at immigration?"

Barb yelled at me, but I took it. "Jesus, Jason, here you are, dragging me halfway across a continent to get married maybe two hours after your brother is killed, and you're asking me whether or not I should have a carry-on bag? So that some customs guy believes that we're going to get married?"

"But we *are* going to get married."

Barb screamed out the window and lit another of many cigarettes. "This is about Cheryl. Isn't it? Tell me – isn't it?"

"Leave Cheryl out of this."

"No. We can't have anyone discussing little Miss Joan of Arc." She threw her cigarette out the window. "Sorry."

"You're right. It does have to do with Cheryl."

"How?"

I didn't say anything.

"How?"

I kept silent.

Barb is a smart woman. She said, "Now I don't know if you're doing me a favor, or if I'm doing *you* one."

140

"You're probably right."

"You're as nuts as your father. You think you're not, but you are."

"What if I am?"

"The harder people try to be the opposite of their parents, the quicker they become them. It's a fact. Now just drive."

"What are we going to tell people when we get back?"

"We're going to tell people I freaked out. We're going to tell them that I went crazy and drove out toward the daffodil farm, and you saw me and followed me, and that I deliberately got lost, and that you had to hunt me down somewhere in all that scuzzy wilderness out there. That's what we're going to tell them."

"But your car is in the garage."

"I'll think of something. Just drive us to the airport."

The airport journey was different from the taxi ride Cheryl and I took in 1988. Back then all the bridges we had to cross seemed exciting, almost like roller coasters. Crossing them with Barb, they were just these things you didn't want to be stuck on during an earthquake.

And of course Kent was dead, too. I tried to speak about him, but Barb would have none of it. "As far as I'm concerned, for the next twelve hours you *are* Kent. Just drive."

We dumped the truck in the long-term parking lot and headed to the terminal. Customs preclearance was a snap. Barb was bawling as she showed them the engagement ring Kent had given her, and they waved us through with Parisian-style shrugs and smiles. The ticket clerk had passed along the message to the flight crew that we were going to get married; inside the plane it was broadcast, and we were upgraded to business class while everybody whistled and cheered, making Barb cry all the harder. The drinks, meanwhile, kept coming and coming, and Barb kept drinking and drinking, and on the ground she was one big wobble; escorting her from one gate to the next at LAX was like trying to propel a shopping cart full of balloons on a windy day, and on the second flight she simply cried for most of the trip. We landed just after midnight.

In the decade since my first trip there, Las Vegas had been rebuilt from the ground up. Pockets of authentic sleaze peeked out here and there, but the city's aura was different, more professional. I could look at all the new casinos and imagine people sinning away like mad, but I could also envision management meetings and cubicles and photocopiers tucked away in the bowels of the recently spruced up casinos.

I asked the driver to take us to the stretch of chapels between Fremont Street and Caesars Palace, a piece of the Strip that had remained unmolested by progress. The chapel where Cheryl and I had been married was still there. I paid the cabbie while Barb got out. We didn't say anything as we went into the chapel, and I was disappointed that the old guy who'd performed the first ceremony was no longer there.

A couple from Oklahoma was in front of us. We witnessed for them, and they witnessed for us, through a secular version of a wedding ceremony that did good service to the term "quickie." Within fifteen minutes we were wed, and another cab drove us to Caesars Palace, which had also been renovated in the intervening decade.

We checked in as husband and wife, and we were walking through the lobby to the elevator bank when we heard someone calling our names. I had the same sick feeling I had when I was twelve and got caught pilfering raspberries from the neighbors' patch. We turned around. It was Rick, this guy I'd gone to high school with. He'd aged faster than most, and was much larger than I'd remembered. His head was shiny.

"Rick. Hey, hi."

"Hi, Jason. Hi, Barb. Jason, I thought you were Kent for a second there. Did all you guys come down together? I can't believe how cheap everything here is during the off-season."

I didn't know how to reply, but Barb said, "I like blackjack, but the guys are more into craps."

Rick said, "I'm a blackjack guy, too. Craps is for the real hotshots. I like to stretch my losses out over a few days so I can savor the experience. When did you guys get here?"

"Just today."

"You're staying at Caesars?"

I said we were.

"I'm at this motel off the Strip. Twenty-nine bucks a night, with free coffee and croissants in the morning. Talk about a deal. You guys want to come play with me?"

I was going to motion to the elevators, but Barb said, "Sure." My eyes must have sprung out of my sockets. "Jason, go upstairs with the others. I'll meet you in a few minutes. I think my luck is changing."

Rick said, "Now, *this* woman has the Vegas spirit. Come on, Barb. I'll show you my lucky table."

Barb said, "I'll be up shortly. Go, Jason."

This was one very screwed-up situation, but the thought of a quiet room was seductive, and I went upstairs. I showered for twenty minutes, and tried to figure out everything that had happened during the day, particularly how we might explain to people how it was that Rick Kozarek saw us in Caesars Palace the night Kent died.

I got out, shivered in the all-powerful air-conditioning and got into bed, awaiting Barb and wondering how Mom was going to take Kent's death. Would she just give up on life altogether?

An hour passed. I put cable news on as wallpaper and dozed off. When Barb came in the door and woke me up, her face was neutral.

"It's about time. It's two-thirty, Barb."

"I'm having a shower."

"You went to play blackjack? Are you out of your mind?"

She said nothing, but emerged from the shower and got into bed with me, and the truth is that from the tension and grief and stress and you-name-it, the sex was a repeat of my marriage to Cheryl. Around six o'clock Barb phoned the concierge for tickets on an 8:10 nonstop to Vancouver. We were silent most of the way home.

It was only in the truck, nearing the house, that I asked, "Barb, by the way, you never did say what made you decide to go play blackjack with Rick Kozarek. That was really random."

"Blackjack? I didn't play blackjack. I killed him."

I nearly put the truck in the ditch as I stopped. "You *what?*"

"There was no other option. He saw the two of us together. He'd have blabbed. So I went back to his motel room with him and cracked him on the back of his head with a forty-ouncer of discount vodka. Done."

"You *murdered* him?"

"Don't be sanctimonious with me, rebel boy. You wanted to get married in Las Vegas, and you got it. And part of the deal of getting married in Las Vegas is that you might very well bump into the Rick Kozareks of this world. Now, are you going to drive me the final block home, or am I going to walk?"

I didn't know what to say, because I was thinking, *Oh, God, this is how my father felt back in 1988.*

So Barb got out of the truck and walked home. The heel of her left shoe was about to come off, and a mist of dandelion fluff had attached itself to her panty hose. I got out and walked alongside her. "Barb, what if you're caught?"

She stopped. "*Caught?* Jason, get real. One of the bonuses of staying in a twenty-nine-dollar-a-night motel room is the convenient lack of surveillance or security. And if I'm caught, I'm caught, but I won't be."

We rounded the corner and there were all Kent's friends' cars, as well as my mother's. Barb and I looked like wrecks – we *were* wrecks – and my distress couldn't have been more visible.

As Barb predicted, she was never caught, and everyone fully bought her story about going crazy – which is, in its way, true. Kent's funeral was four days later, and that was that.

A month later, my mother phoned to say that Barb was pregnant with twins. And maybe another month later I bumped into Stacy Kozarek, Rick's sister, in the Lonsdale Public Market, where she was buying clams. She told me that Rick had been found murdered in his motel room, and the Las Vegas police thought it was somehow gang-related.

*   *   *

And there you go.

I'm looking out the pickup truck's window at Ambleside Beach and the ocean and the freighters – at the mothers tending to their children covered in sand and sugar and spit, at the blue sky and the mallard ducks and the Canada geese. And Joyce is smiling at me. Dogs indeed smile, and Joyce has every reason to smile. It's a beautiful world and she's part of it – and yet . . .

. . . and yet we humans are *not* a part of it.

Look at us. We're all born lost, aren't we? We're all born separated from God – over and over life makes sure to inform us of this – and yet we're all *real*: we have *names*, we have *lives*. We mean something. We *must*. My heart is so cold. And I feel so lost. I shed my block of hate but what if nothing emerges to fill in the hole it left? The universe is so large, and the world is so glorious, but here I am on a sunny August morning with chilled black ink pumping through my veins, and I feel like the unholiest thing on earth.

This letter is now going into the safety deposit box. Happy birthday, my sons. You're men now, and this is the way the world works.

Part Three

2002: Heather

Saturday afternoon 4:00

I met Jason in a line-up at Toys R Us. He was in front of me buying a pile of toys, looking slightly sad, slightly damaged and slightly naughty. I had some toy plastic groceries for my sister's kid, who never really cares what I give her, and I just wanted to escape the store. But instead there's this sad guy in front of me – no wedding ring, straight looking, and no apparent tattoos – and so maybe I didn't want to leave too quickly after all.

The cashier was changing the paper tape – why does that always happen in my line? Standing on the counter was a plastic giraffe model someone had abandoned. Some wise-acre had strapped it into a little sheepskin coat with a fleece lining; it probably came from the box of one of Barbie's gay boyfriends.

I said, "I think our giraffe here is a bit sexually conflicted."

Jason said, "It's that fleece-lined bomber jacket – always a dead giveaway."

"Manly, and yet more like a prop than a garment."

"I bet you anything our giraffe friend here is always buying Shetland sweaters for the younger giraffes, but he doesn't even understand why he does it."

"The sweater-buying impulse baffles him more than it frightens him."

Jason handed his toys to the cashier. "He's, like, a vice president of Nestlé operating out of Switzerland, but he's totally clueless, and he always misses the parts of the board meetings where they do all the evil stuff to third world countries. He sort of bumbles into the boardroom and everyone indulges him . . ."

"His name is Gerard."

Jason said, "Yes. Gerard T. Giraffe."

"What does the 'T' stand for?"

" 'The.' "

We rang our toys through the till and kept right on talking. I don't even know who was steering whom, but we ended up in the Denny's next door, and we kept expanding Gerard's universe. Jason said Gerard had this real fixation about being manly. "He wears the sheepskin coat as much as he can. He worships George Peppard, and buys old black-and-white photos and scrapbooks about him on eBay."

"And he decorated his apartment in rich tobacco browns and somber ochers in maybe 1975 and has never changed them."

"Yes. Manly colors. Burly walnut furniture."

"Hai Karate aftershave."

"Yeah, yeah – he still uses words like 'aftershave.' "

"And he invites his friends over for dinner parties, but

the food is from some other period in history. Cherries Jubilee."

"Baked Alaska."

"T-bone steaks."

"Fondue."

I asked, "What are his friends' names?"

"Chester. Roy. And Alphonse – Alphonse is the exotic one with a hint of 'the dance' in his past. And Francesca, the beautiful but broke fifth daughter of a disgraced Rust Belt vacuum cleaner tycoon."

"Possibly someone, Francesca even, is wearing a cravat."

I thought Jason was the most talkative man I'd ever met, but I later found out he'd said more to me in those two hours than he'd spoken to all the people in his life in the past decade. He was obviously a born talker, but he needed a ventriloquist's dummy to speak through. Somehow that dorky giraffe on the counter had pressed his ON button, and we had just invented the first of a set of what I would call fusion entities – characters, that could only exist when the two of us were together.

I asked, "What kind of car would Gerard drive?"

"Car? That's simple. A 1973 Ford LTD Brougham sedan with a claret-colored vinyl roof, white leather interior and opera windows."

"Perfect."

In the end, I think the relationships that survive in this world are the ones where the two people can finish each other's sentences. Forget drama and torrid sex and the clash of opposites. Give me banter any day of the week. And our characters were the best banterers going.

When Jason left to go pick up his nephews that day,

he took my number with him and called me, and that was that.

*   *   *

Barb just phoned. She's arrived in Redwood City, south of San Francisco, where she works with Chris – Cheryl's brother. *The* Cheryl. I'm no dum-dum on the score, but Jason and Cheryl was so long ago. We move on, or rather, Jason sure tries.

Barb's commuting down the coast, and she asked me to baby-sit the twins for a few days. Chris proposed to her last week, and she accepted; the world moves in mysterious ways – I mean, Cheryl Anway's *brother* and Jason Klaasen's *sister-in-law*.

Chris creates face-mapping software programs for governments and big business. Chris can take your face, pinpoint your nostrils, the ends of your lips, your retinas, and with a few more measurements generate your unique unchangeable face-map. You can't fake a face, even with cosmetic surgery. It all seems a bit spooky to me. I mean, this could be abused *so* easily, and I told Chris so when he was over at our place for dinner.

"Chris, what if you took the face of a famous actor, and entered their facial proportions into your database – would you find their . . . duplicate?"

"The term we use is 'analog.'"

"Come again?"

"Your analog isn't your twin or your clone. He or she is the person out there who's maybe a millimeter away from having the same face as you."

"You're joking."

"Not at all. But the weird thing is, an analog doesn't even

have to be the same sex, let alone the same hair color or skin color. Put you and your analog into a room together and people are going to assume the two of you are twins. If you're a boy and she's a girl, people will simply assume it's your twin in drag."

"This exists?"

"The government already has face-maps of all prison inmates and other people who float through the judicial system."

Barb was particularly intrigued by this idea. Jason's father had made some very badly chosen comments about the twins at Kent's memorial a few years back, and since then she's been on a crusade to learn everything about twins she can. She began to discuss using face-maps to help twins who've been separated when very young, and where the law prevents them from accessing closed files. She became passionate, and there's nothing sexier than enthusiasm, and boy did Chris respond. First, he got her a job at his company's Vancouver affiliate, and now they're engaged.

There's a lesson there.

I'm sitting here inputting this in Barb's home office beside the kitchen, looking around at all the bits of things that make her house a home: flowers; a regularly culled cork notice board; obviously tended-to IN and OUT baskets; framed family photos (where does she get the energy to frame things – how does *anybody* get the energy to frame things?); clean rugs – it's a long list. I love Jason dearly, but neither of us is very gifted on the domestic front. We're not quite as bad as those people who plaster a Union Jack or a Confederate flag up on the windows as curtains, and Molly Maid comes in once a month to decontaminate the place with industrial vacuums and cleaning agents perfected during the Vietman War. It's always hard for us afterward to make eye contact with the disgusted Russian and Honduran girls who do the place. Is it so wrong to be a slob?

*　　*　　*

Okay, I know I'm using both the present and past tenses for Jason and me. Is he alive or dead? I have no choice but to hope he's somewhere and breathing. He's been gone a few months now. Not a peep. He went down to buy smokes at Mac's Milk and never came home. He walked – no car involved – and, well, the thing about people vanishing is that they've *vanished*. They haven't left you a clue. They're *gone*. A clue? I'd kill for a clue. I'd sell my retinas for a clue. But "vanish" is indeed the correct verb here.

It's . . .

The phone. I have to answer it.

*　　*　　*

That was Reg, calling from his apartment over near Lonsdale. He just wanted to talk. Jason's disappearance has left him as bewildered as it's left me. And I must say, it truly is hard to imagine Reg as the ogre Jason's always made him out to be.

Okay, Heather, be honest. You *know* darn well why Reg changed: losing Jason was the clincher. He also got royally dumped, just after Jason disappeared – by Ruth, this woman he'd been seeing for years. And not only was he dumped, but she really laid into him when she did the dumping. The essence of her farewell speech (delivered in a Keg steak restaurant as a neutral space) was that Reg was the opposite of everything he thought he was: cruel instead of kind; blind instead of wise; not tough but with skin as thin as frost. I didn't like Ruth much the few times we met; she had judgment written all over her face. In real life, it's always the judgmental people who get caught robbing the choirboys' charity raffle fund.

I think I'm the sole mortal friend or contact Reg still has, which is odd, as I'm not at all churchy. He sure doesn't have friends at work; the day Ruth dumped him, he was rummaging in the plastic spoon drawer in the coffee room, and found a voodoo doll of himself covered with pins made from straightened paper clips; the head had been burned a few times.

"Heather." The sound of his voice just now – his soul was sore.

"Reg. How're you doing?"

Pause. "Okay. But just okay."

"I haven't heard anything from the RCMP today."

"I doubt we will."

"Don't be so glum. Don't. And you know what? Chris has mapped Jason's face from an old photo. So at least he's in that index now."

"Heather, how many people are in that index, anyway?"

"I don't know. Maybe a few hundred thousand. But it's a start."

"*Fah*. A few hundred thousand . . ."

"Reg, don't be so negative. It's a start. And the index is only ever going to grow."

"He's gone."

"No, he's not *gone*, Reg."

"He is."

I lost it here. I said, "Reg, you either have to have some hope here, or you stop calling, okay?"

Reg was silent, and then: "Sorry."

"It's hard on all of us."

"Heather?"

"Yes."

"Let me ask you a question . . ."

"Okay. Shoot."

"If you could be God for a day, would you rule the world any differently from the way it's being run now?"

"Reg, you know I'm weak on religion."

"Well, *would* you?"

"Reg, have you eaten lunch? You need to eat."

"You didn't answer my question. If you were God, would you rule the world any differently?"

Would I? "No."

"Why not?"

"Reg, the world is the way it is because – well, because *that's the way it is*."

"Meaning?"

"Reg, Jason and I once discussed this. Sometimes I think God is like weather – you may not like the weather, but it has nothing to do with you. You just happen to be there. Deal with it. Sadness and grief are part of being human and always will be. Who would I be to fix that?"

"I forget that sometimes. Me, of all people. I take things too personally." He went quiet again, then: "How are the boys?"

"They're downstairs, wasted on sugar. Kelly from next door gave them KitKats, and I could just throttle the woman."

Reg was fishing here. "Reg," I asked, "would you like to come over for dinner? It's five o'clock already." He paused just long enough to make a dinnertime call seem casual. And so he's coming tonight for dinner, around eight, and I just heard one of the twins crying downstairs . . .

Saturday afternoon 6:30

Sometimes I think the only way to deal with turbocharged kids is to give them even more sugar and lock them in a room with a TV set. As I know zilch about kids, this is my first (and last) means of coping, and it seems to work just fine.

I was setting the table when I heard a cartoon bird character on the TV squawk – and suddenly I was back on my first official date with Jason. I thought I'd jot it down here quickly.

The day after we met, Jason and I were headed to look at birds in the pet shop at Park Royal – he was thinking of buying a pair of sulfur-crested cockatiels – but in the store I had a rapid-onset itching fit, allergies, and I had to get some cortisone for my elbows. I work as a court stenographer and am somewhat in public all day, so my skin needs to be in relatively okay shape, and lately my eczema has been a real problem.

So we were standing at the counter at London Drugs when I burst into tears. Jason asked me what was wrong, and I told the truth, which was that it was the most unromantic beginning of a date with the most lovable guy I'd ever met. He told me I was being silly, and gave me our first kiss, right there in line-up.

He didn't get any birds, but he did buy me three small, anatomically correct rubber frogs, the size of canapés, who soon became Froggles, Walter and Benihana, three more characters for our imaginary universe.

I must be coming across as a basket case here. Frogs and giraffes and . . . Well, we all create our private worlds between us, don't we? Most couples I know have an insider's secret language, even if it's just their special nicknames for the salt and pepper shakers. After a while, our characters were so finely honed that they could have had their own theme parks in Japan, Europe and the U.S. Sunbelt, as well as merchandise outlets in the malls. After his life of silence, I think that our characters were Jason's liberation.

And now I think I have to start preparing dinner. God bless Barb's copper-bottomed pots and her spice rack of the gods.

Saturday night 10:30

Okay, Barb's housekeeper will be in at 8:30 tomorrow to clean up the battlefield. I really ought to have known better than to put the twins at the same table as Reg, who's too old and too set in his ways to be comfortable around young children. He tried to keep it together for my sake, but the twins tonight would have worn out an East German ladies' weight-lifting coach circa 1971. They were *monsters*. In the end I caved in and gave them Jell-O, then packed them off to watch TV. Barb is going to have my head on a block for teaching them such bad habits.

The good part was that once the kids were bundled off, Reg relaxed and got a bit drunk and picked away at his fettuccine. Jason always told me Reg never drank, but then Jason didn't see his father for so many years. . . . In any event, Reg drank white wine, not red, and then tested my grounding in reality by bringing out a *cigarette* and smoking it as if he'd been born to the task.

"Smoking now?"

"Might as well. Always wondered what it was like."

"What is it like?"

He chuckled. "Addictive."

"There you go."

I bummed a cigarette from him and smoked for the first time in twenty years and got the nicotine dizzies. I felt like a schoolgirl. When you conspire with someone like Reg, you feel as if you're committing one serious transgression.

Soon enough the conversation turned to Reg's sorrow about his lost boys – Kent the minor deity and his awful senseless death, and then Jason, but after three months there's simply no new ground to cover. I had the feeling that what we were discussing tonight is almost exactly what we'll be discussing in a decade.

Reg became morose. "I just don't understand – the most wretched people in this world prosper, while the innocent and the devout get only suffering."

"Reg, you can spend all night – and the rest of your life, for that matter – looking for some little equation that makes it all equate, but I don't think that equation exists. The world is the world. All you can change is the way you deal with what's thrown your way."

Reg sloshed around the last bit of wine in his glass, then knocked it back. "But it's hard."

"It is, Reg."

He looked so damn sad. Jason quite resembles his father; I almost wonder if they'd be analogs of each other, but tonight there was something new in his face. "Reg . . . ?"

"Yes, Heather."

"Do you ever have doubts about . . . the things you believe in?"

He looked up from his glass. "If you'd asked me that a decade ago, I'd have turned purple and cast you out of my house – or whatever house we were in. I'd have seen you as a corrupting influence. I'd have scorned you. But here I am now, and all I can do is say *yes*, which doesn't even burn or sting. I feel so heavy, I feel like barbells. I feel like I just want to melt into the planet, like a boulder in a swamp, and be done with everything."

"Reg, I'm going to tell you a story, okay?"

"A story? Sure. What about?"

I couldn't believe I was saying the words, but here I was. "About something stupid and crazy I did last week. I haven't told anyone about it, and if I don't tell someone I'm going to explode. Will you listen?"

"You always listen to me."

I twiddled a noodle coated with cold Parmesan cheese, and said, "Last week I phoned Chris, down in California."

"He's a good boy."

"He is."

"Why did you call?"

"I wanted to – *needed* to – ask him a favor."

"What was it?"

"I asked him to give me the names and addresses of the people who made the closest match to Jason in the facial profiling index."

"And?"

"And . . . there was this one guy who lives in South Carolina, named Terry, who's about seventy-five years old, and then there was this other guy, Paul, who lives down in Beaverton, Oregon, near Portland. A suburb."

"Go on."

"Well, it turns out this Paul guy has a long but minor record – a few stolen cars – and he got caught fencing memory chips in northern California."

"You went down there to meet him, didn't you?"

*   *   *

Oh, Heather, you knew it wouldn't be a good thing.

I drove down I–5 to Beaverton, an eight-hour trip in migraine-white sun, my sunglasses forgotten back on the kitchen counter. In Washington state my body started to unravel: my elbows began crusting with eczema just north of Seattle; by the time I reached Olympia, I felt as if my arms were caked in dried mud. I cried most of the way down – I wasn't a pretty picture. People who drove past me and saw me at the wheel must have said to themselves, *Boy, sometimes life is rough,* and they'd be glad they weren't me.

I found a chain motel on the outskirts of Portland and spent an hour in a scratchy-bottomed bathtub, listening to teenagers party one room over. I was trying to rinse the road trip out of my body, as well as build up the courage to go knocking on this Paul guy's door. I was expecting him to inhabit a mobile home that listed on three wheels, with a one-eyed pit bull and a girlfriend armed with a baseball bat and incisors loaded with vinegar – and this was pretty close. I mean, *what* was I *thinking*? I'm just this broad who comes out of nowhere, who knocks on this guy's flaking red-painted front door in the dead-yellow-lawn part of town at 9:45 at night. When the door opened, I was struck dumb, because there before me was Jason – but *not* Jason – hair too dark, maybe a few years older, and with bigger eyebrows, but it seemed like his essence was there.

"Uh, can I help you? *Ma'am?*"

I sniffled. I hadn't planned for this moment, and the resemblance to Jason stopped me cold, even though it was the reason for my mission.

He said, "Okay. I know what this is. You're Alex's cupcake looking to get his leaf blower back. Well, tell that cheap bastard that until I see my cooler chest and all the beer that was in it, he's not gonna see his leaf blower." Paul's voice was higher than Jason's; no similarity there.

"I – "

"Huh? What?"

"I don't know anybody named Alex."

"Okay, then, lady, who are you? Because I've got *Jurassic Park III* on pause, and if I start watching it again right now, I'll have just enough time to finish before Sheila gets back from Tae Bo."

"I'm Heather."

Paul looked back at the TV and zapped it off with the remote.

"Heather, do I know you or something? Wait – are you Sheila's crazy half-sister? Just what I need. She said you were in Texas for good."

I couldn't speak, because I was looking at Jason hidden somewhere not far beneath Paul's bone structure.

He said, "So what's the score here? I stopped dealing years ago, so don't even try me there. And if you're here for money, you're at the wrong place."

"I'm not here for anything, Paul. I'm not."

"Yeah. Right."

"No – " I hadn't given this part any real thought, or rather, I'd assumed it would be magic and not need any planning.

"I'm waiting."

I said, "My boyfriend's been missing for three months now, and I don't know what I'm going to do, I miss him so much, and I'm so desperate, and I was able to tap into the government's database of criminal faces, so I did, and I found yours, because you're the one closest to him, and I came down here to – " I lost it here.

"You *what*?"

I was crying and looking at the ground where the dead yellow lawn met the concrete. "I came here to see if you were like him."

"Are you out of your tree, lady?"

"I'm not 'lady.' My name is Heather."

"*Heather,* are you out of your tree?"

I was choking and even more of a mess.

"Heather, sit down. Jesus."

I sat down. He leaned against the railing and lit up a cigarette the same way Jason did. "You can really do that – just go into a computer and find the person who looks like you?"

I honked my nose. "Welcome to the future. Yes. You can."

"*Whoa.*" He spent a moment obviously contemplating the social ramifications of analogs. I was realizing what a mistake this had been.

"So," he said, "do I?"

"Do you what?"

"Look like him. Your boyfriend."

My body, drained of stress, went limp. I was already driving back up the coast in my head. "Yeah. Pretty much. Not quite twins, but with different hair, three months of dieting, and some tweezers, you could pull it off."

"Huh."

"I should go."

"No. Don't. I'll get you a beer."

"I'm driving."

"So?"

I didn't argue. Paul went into the house and brought me back a can of something and opened it for me. Chivalry. To be honest, I wanted to see his face again. He'd had acne as a teenager, he'd spent too much time in the sun, he had twenty extra pounds, and he had a Celtic cross tattooed on his left shoulder, but it was all mesmerizingly Jason-ish.

"He dumped you?"

"*No.*"

"Sorry. I've gotta ask these things."

We looked at each other.

"So tell me where it is you're supposed to go to find your twin?"

"Your analog."

"Huh?"

"That's what you are. You're an analog of my boyfriend."

"So where do I go to find my analog?"

"You don't. I just fluked out. I have a friend of a friend who works in the place where the facial data's stored." He sat down beside me – too close beside me – on the crumbling concrete front steps. He touched the small of my back and I jumped out of my skin, at which point a black martial-artsy club smacked him on his forehead. It was Sheila.

"You stinking son of a dog – "

"Sheila – this isn't what it looks like."

I ran for my car, and luckily Sheila ignored me. Paul still must have a goose egg on his forehead, and I doubt Sheila's ever going to believe his story. On the other hand, Reg thought it was kind of funny, which made me feel better.

Saturday night 11:45

It's almost midnight, and the kids have finally passed out from sugar fatigue. They must be diabetic by now.

I spend my life in court hearing people yammer away and for once I want to be on the stand. Forget my crazy trip to Portland. I want to talk about what happened *yesterday,* because that's what's gotten me to writing here. I'd have told Reg, but I have a hunch he doesn't go in for this kind of stuff.

But first, you have to understand that my life before Jason was dull. Not insignificant, mind you, but not many kicks either. I grew up in North Van, seven years ahead of Jason. Have I mentioned that I'm seven years older than he is? At the time of the Delbrook Massacre I was living in Ontario and had just earned all the papers I needed to be a court stenographer. I was already working part time, in Windsor – a friend got me a job there. I was always a good typist, but stenography? It works by phonetics, not letters, and when it's flowing properly, it's as if the things people are telling each other in court are emerging from my own brain in real time. It's like I'm inventing the world! Other stenographers say the same thing – it's like catching the perfect wave. And it's funny, because one of the side effects of being a good stenographer is that you can tell right away when someone's fibbing. Oh yeah: the presiding judge and jury might miss it, but not *this* gal. I suppose if you asked me what was the one thing that made me different from all other people, that might be it – that I'm a living lie detector.

That's how I "met" Jason the first time. On TV back in the 1980s; he was at a press conference just after he'd been absolved of any wrongdoing. I was homesick in Windsor, watching TV at my place with two neighbors who were also from Vancouver. We were drinking beer and feeling alienated from the massive quilt of autumn leaves outside. My neighbors said Jason was lying his ass off, but I said no way, and I stuck up for him, even back then. Imagine telling the truth about something as gruesome as that massacre, and having only half the world believe you; I don't think you could ever trust people again. So when I encountered Jason at the Toys R Us, he looked familiar as well as sad, but at first I couldn't peg why.

But I was going to discuss Friday. It's what started me going on this. I was downtown on my lunch break from the courthouse. I was in a drugstore getting a few things for this weekend with the kids. My cell phone battery was dead, so I went to a pay phone and checked my messages, and there was just one, a woman's voice – nice enough, maybe fiftyish – and she had something to tell me she said was both unusual and urgent. And then she hung up, no phone number or anything. Well what was I supposed to make of *that*? I listened to the message again. She didn't sound evil, and believe me, I've seen and heard so much evil in the courtroom that by now you could use my blood as an anti-evil vaccine. Who was this woman, and what exactly was she on about – telemarketing?

If it had been something to do with Jason, I figured she would have used a different voice with a different tone. *Meaning what, Heather?* Meaning, this woman didn't sound like the type to deliver ransom instructions or notify the cops to go looking in the Fraser River for a corpse rolled up in a discount Persian carpet. I know that voice, and it wasn't hers.

So I spent the rest of the afternoon slightly distracted, trying to pinpoint the nature of her voice, in the process even making some boo-boos on the court transcript – but it's a dull-as-dishwater property suit, and the chances of anyone consulting the record are zero. I could sit there pumping out the Girl Guide Pledge all afternoon, and nobody would ever know. This is both a plus and a minus of my job: my work is important, and yet it isn't. To be honest, they should just wire everybody up, stuff the room with cameras and fire me, except that the electronics would cost far more to maintain and service. So my job's safe for a while yet.

At five o'clock, I made the dash across the bridge and got to Barb's just in time to take charge of the twins as Barb raced out to the airport. The two boys were ravenous. Dinner became the next thing, and then they wanted to show me their computer games, which was a snoozer for me, and then I headed back to the kitchen for a sip of white wine and my first calm moment since the morning.

I phoned and checked my messages. None. So I call-forwarded my number to Barb's and sat at the kitchen table where I picked at the kids' leftover hot dogs and tried to enjoy the silence. Then the phone rang. It was the woman.

"Hello, is this . . . Heather?"

"Yes, it is. Who's this?" I kept my tone friendly.

"I'm Allison."

"Hello, Allison. You're the one who said you had some information for me?"

"Well, I do and I don't."

"You're losing me."

"Do you have five minutes?"

What the heck. "Sure." I poured another glass and sat on the bar stool by the flecked black marble counter.

"I guess I should tell you right off, Heather, I'm a psychic."

I was about to hang up.

"Don't hang up."

"You're a good psychic. You read my mind."

"No. It's common sense. I'd hang up, too, if some woman saying she was a psychic called me."

"Allison, I'm sure you're a nice person, but . . ."

"Oh, I say."

"What?"

"*Oh, I say.*"

"Oh, I say" was Gerard T. Giraffe's unfunny entrance line, like the ones people have in sitcoms which are supposed to be funny, but really aren't, like when Norm enters the bar on *Cheers,* and everyone says, "Norm!" She was even using the correct Gerard tone of voice, baritone and bumbling.

"'*Oh, I say*' . . . Does that mean anything to you?"

I kept silent.

"'Oh, I say.'"

"Who are you, Allison? What do you want?"

"I don't want anything. I don't. But all day I've been getting this voice coming through my brain in the middle of whatever I'm doing, saying 'Oh, I say,' and it's freaking me out, and I'm supposed to be used to this sort of thing."

"How did you connect the voice to my name?"

"That's almost the easiest part. I emptied my head and used a pencil on white paper in a dark room and your name and number came out. It's not too far a stretch to get a phone number when you get such a weird, specific message like 'Oh, I say' delivered in a Rex Harrison baritone."

"Why are you doing this?"

"Heather, I'm sorry you feel this way. But there's no game-playing going on here. I don't want money. I don't want anything. But there's still these words pumping out of wherever. I just want to make sure I'm not cracking up. Oh, I say. Oh, I say. Oh, I say."

I was silent. In the other room the kids were bickering.

"Heather, look. I've never told anyone this before, but I'm not really a psychic. I'm a fake psychic. I look at people's faces, their jewelry and scars and footwear and shirts and you name it. I pretty much feed them what they want to hear. You don't even need too much intuition to do it. I'm surprised there aren't millions of psychics out there. It's a total racket."

So much for me being a living lie detector. "How can you mess with people's lives like that?"

"Messing? Not at all. I give them hope, and I never raise their expectations too high. The only thing most people want is a bit of proof, however flimsy, that people they once knew are thinking of them from the great beyond."

"Most people? What do the other people want?"

"They want a conversation with the dead, but I can't do that for them. Because I'm a fake. And even if I could, a conversation with someone in the great beyond might not be the smartest thing to facilitate."

"But you're a fake. You said so yourself."

"I am, Heather. But this 'Oh, I say' thing – it's the only potentially real signal I've ever picked up on my antenna, and frankly it's scaring me."

"What do you want me to do?"

"Just tell me that it means something – that it means something real."

"Allison, give me a second here."

I put the wineglass down on the counter. There were lipstick stains on it. Why was I wearing lipstick to baby-sit the kids? The icemaker rumbled and stopped, and the fridge's humming entered second gear.

"Okay," I said, "It means something."

"Oh, thank God."

"Wait. Hold on a minute. When you get your messages or whatever, is it a voice in your head? Or is it like a text message on a computer screen?"

"It's sort of both and neither. It's more a thing that passes through you, like when you leave the house and you realize the stove is still on. It defies words, and yet at the same time, it *is* words."

That sounded real enough. "Do you see his face?"

"No. But I can definitely feel him near."

"So you can't tell me what he looks like – it's not like I want proof – I'm just curious."

"Okay. I'd say he's taller than you – six something – mouse-brown hair, not thinning, gray-green eyes. That's not much to go by. I could have made that up."

"It's close. Very close." It was bang on.

Allison asked, "What does it mean, then? It's a weird message."

"I can't tell you."

"Okay. Fair enough."

"Tell me, Allison, does a person have to be dead in order to send you voices or words?"

"From what I've read, not necessarily."

"Does this voice say anything else to you?"

"No. Not words."

"What do you mean, 'not words'?"

"Just what I said. The voice – male, fifties maybe? – says 'Oh I say,' and then there's this weird laughter. But it's not like real laughter. It's fake."

"Oh, Jesus." I put the phone down. I could hear Allison on the other end calling "Heather? Heather? Heather?"

"Allison, where are you calling from? What's your number?"

She gave it to me. I asked if we could meet soon. She couldn't make it today, so tomorrow it is – in the morning, down at the beach.

It was bedtime. We'd see what tomorrow would bring.

Sunday afternoon 3:30

Oh Lord. What am I to do? I arranged to meet her at the fish-and-chips stand between Ambleside Beach and the soccer field. Jason always liked going there, so I figured it would increase the chance of a Jason vibe. Did I just write the word "vibe"? I hope that doesn't betoken the start of something bad. I was bleary-eyed and freezing, and the twins didn't seem to notice or care – oh, to be young and have a proper thermostat again. So I waited for this Allison woman.

The stand was closed, and we were alone save for a few unambitious seagulls trolling the metal litter drums for snacks. The air was salty and nice, clean smelling. I turned to look at the waves, at the little tips of whitecaps, and I turned around, and there was Allison, older than I'd thought, about sixty, and smaller too, her body like a pit inside a large prune of teal-green fleece and zippers. She wore tight black leggings so maybe she was a walker. Do I care? Yes. I care. This woman was my lifeline.

"Allison?"

"Heather?"

"I'm glad you could come meet me here."

Allison said, "How could I miss it? This is the first interesting thing to happen in my life since my husband died."

"I'm sorry to hear that."

"Don't be. It was horrible for him. When he went it was a blessing."

"Is that when you first decided to try your hand at being psychic?"

"At first. I missed him like I'd miss sight or taste or hearing – he was an extra sense for me. I felt like I'd been blinded. I wanted him returned to me any way I could manage."

We all walked toward the soccer field. "What happened then?"

"First I went to other so-called psychics; they all checked me out and picked up on the fact that I'd recently lost Glenn. Something in my eyes, or maybe the fact that I hadn't bothered to pretty myself up. I know all the signs now.

172

These psychics would mostly milk Glenn's death – 'I think it was a quick death – no! It was a slow death. He wanted you to be brave and not to worry.' None of it was of any consequence, but it made me feel good at a time when other things weren't working. You don't need to be a psychic to know that, but when the message comes from the spirit world, *wow,* you almost swoon from the illusion of contact."

"Why did you decide to do it yourself? Don't you think it's sort of mean for pseudo-psychics to lead people on?"

"Mean? No. Like I told you last night, it's harmless stuff, and even the worst psychic made me feel a heckuva lot better than all the Wellbutrin or Tia Maria I swallowed. Psychics are no different from quack vitamins or aromatherapy or any of that stuff you see ads for. And I'll tell you this: When people come to me, I really do help them. And you'd be amazed at the problems everybody has."

"I work as a court stenographer. I think I see more problems than most people."

It was becoming windy, and our voices were being swept away. Allison said to me, "Heather, please don't tell me anything about yourself. Please. If I'm going to be genuinely psychic here, I don't want the results to be influenced."

Just then the kids found a dead crow and shouted, "Aunt Heather!" and I looked at Allison and said, "Well, now you know at least that much."

I suggested we go talk someplace warm. We went to the café adjacent to the ball pit at Park Royal mall, where the twins romped among filthy colored-plastic balls with germ loads reminiscent of the Black Plague.

Allison said, "I'll be frank with you. I don't know if you're married or single or divorced or lesbian or anything else. And I'll say it again: I don't know where I got these voices, or why."

She paused. I tried to conceal my hunger for more contact from Jason. "Allison, did you get any more, uh, messages last night or this morning?"

Allison said, "I did. One."

"What was it?"

She sighed. "I can tell you, if you like, but I have no idea what it means."

"What is it? What did you hear?"

She screwed up her head as if she was about to sing an aria, but instead she spoke in a high, cartoonish voice: "Hey! I'm in dreamland and I got the best table here." She repeated the phrase and then relaxed her head. "That's what I heard."

"Hey, I'm in dreamland and I got the best table here" was a running gag of Froggles, which we used at night before going to sleep. Hearing the words made me high and low at the same time, like a cough syrup high. My face felt like it was morphing into some other face, and my emotions were trying to escape through my bones.

Allison asked me, "Shall I say it for you again?"

"No!" I fairly yelled. I asked Allison to watch the kids for me and I ran out of the small café area beside the pit and headed to the bathroom, where I sat for ten minutes and cried. It's a credit to the human race that several women knocked gently on the door and asked if there was anything they could do. But there wasn't. I sat on the toilet and finally realized that Jason is probably dead; to keep thinking otherwise is simply delusional. The *effort* I've been putting in, being the rock, keeping it together for the sake of Barb, the kids, Reg and Jason's mom. Nobody else has to go back to an apartment where there's a man's wallet with credit cards collecting dust on the counter by the banana bowl, or a bar of orange English soap that's begun to crack beside the bathroom window. I've been trying to keep Jason's aura alive, but every night after work I walk into that apartment and it's leaked away just that much more. His clothes don't look like they're ever going to be worn again, but I can't give them away. So I keep his stuff there. I dust his shoes so they don't look . . . *dead*. I keep his wallet beside the fruit bowl because it looks casual, so when he returns he can say, "Ha-ha, there's my wallet!"

Just listen to me. I'm crazy. I wasn't going to let this happen to me. I wasn't. I was going to be cool, but that's not an option anymore.

Finally, Allison knocked on the stall door. She said she was sorry, but she had to leave. I asked her not to, but she said she didn't have a choice. "I told the girl at the ball pit entryway to keep the kids there until you return."

"Thanks."

*   *   *

I am not a stupid woman. I am aware that there is a world out there that functions without regard to me. There are wars and budgets and bombings and vast dimensions of wealth and greed and ambition and corruption. And yet I don't feel a part of that world, and I wouldn't know how to join if I tried. I live in a condo in a remote suburb of a remote city. It rains a lot here. I need groceries and I go to the shopping center. Sometimes they'll be rebuilding a road and putting those bright blue plastic pipes down in holes; there'll be various grades of gravel in conical piles, and I almost short-circuit when I think of all the systems that are in place to keep our world moving. Where does all the gravel come from? Where do they make blue plastic pipes? Who dug the holes? How did it reach the point where everyone agreed to be doing this? Airports almost make me speechless, what with all of these people in little jumpsuits eagerly bopping about doing some highly qualified task. I don't know how the world works, only that it seems to do so, and I leave it at that.

Sunday night 7:00

Barb gets home in a few minutes. From now on I'll have to write this using my Soviet coal-powered Windows system. I also phoned Reg, and asked him to come for a late dinner at my place tonight. I feel like I need family. My immediate family's all over the country, so Jason's family will do in a pinch. I'd like to be able to call Jason's mother at the extended-care facility, but . . . when she's on, she's great, but when she's off – which is nearly all the time now – I might as well be talking to a tree with its branches flapping in a storm.

No friends to visit. They're either married and moved away, or single and moved away. I could phone them, but they're spooked by Jason's vanishing. They feel sorry for me. They don't know how to discuss it, and when they phone, I'm wondering if they get a poor-Heather thrill at the fact he's still missing.

Any news?
Nope.
None?
Nope.

Oh. So, um – what are you up to lately?
You know. Work.
Oh.
Well . . .
See you one of these days.
'Bye.

*   *   *

I've gone through my memory with a lice comb, and I still can't find any evidence that Jason was connected to ugliness or violence that might in some way have led to his disappearance. I've seen killers galore in the courtroom, and despite all of those he-was-just-a-quiet-man-a-perfect-neighbor things you hear on TV, the fact is that killers have a deadness in their eyes. Their souls are gone, or they've been replaced with something else, like in a body-snatcher movie. I was always happy to be invisible in a courtroom when a murder trial was happening, but it was always the killers who tried hardest to make eye contact with me. During a month-long trial I'd typically look in their direction just one time, and there they were, meeting my glance head on. So no, Jason was no killer. I knew his eyes. He had a fine soul.

Did Jason have a secret life before me? No, nothing scary. He was a contractor's assistant. He picked up drywall, he cut tiles, and he did wiring. His friends weren't truly friends but glorified barflies. The more they wanted to know about the massacre, the less Jason spoke with them. I'm sure they must have been spooked by this, but nobody was ever surprised. His boss, Les, was a good-time Charlie whose wife, Kim, monitored him like the CIA. We had a few barbecues and company picnics together. Les is about as dangerous as a squeak toy.

I tried asking Jason to open up about his past. This was surprisingly hard to do. I know that most guys aren't talkative about themselves, but Jason, good God, it was like pulling teeth out of Mount Rushmore getting him to tell me what he did before he got hired by Les. He'd been working in a kitchen-cupboard-door factory, it turned out.

"Jason, my two cousins work for Canfor's wood panel division. What's the big deal?"

"Nothing."

I pushed and prodded and pleaded, and finally it turned out he was ashamed because he'd only taken a factory job so that he wouldn't have to speak with people during work.

"There's nothing wrong with that, Jason."

"I went for almost four years without having a real conversation with any other human being."

"I – "

"It's true. And I'm not the only one. Those guys you see driving in trucks and wearing hardhats and all of that, they're doing the exact same thing that I was doing. They want to get to the grave without ever having to discuss anything more complex than the hockey pool."

"Jason, that's cynical and simply not true."

"Is it?"

Was it?

Getting Jason to discuss Reg was easy. All I had to do was say that Jason's mom saw Reg in the magazine shop on Lonsdale. Instantly: "That sanctimonious bastard sold me to his God for three beans. That mean, sour freak. He should rot."

"Jason. He can't be all that bad."

"Bad? He's the opposite of everything he claims to be."

Is he?
No.

Sunday night 11:00

The sky was orange-before-the-dark, and I was in the vestibule organizing all of Jason's rubber workboots when Reg showed up. Pathetically, I was hoping the boots' odor might remind me of Jason. Reg's knock was startling, and when I answered the door, Reg looked at my face, and I could see he knew I'd given finally given up hope.

In the kitchen he put on a pot of water for tea and took Jason's wallet from beside the fruit bowl. He removed the contents item by item, laying them out on the countertop.

"So there he is." Laid out were Jason's driver's license, his North Van library card, his Save-On-Foods discount card and some photos of Barb, the kids and me. Reg said, "Heather, something happened today. Tell me what it was." He took the water off the stove before it screamed. He didn't want any extra drama.

I remember reading somewhere that devoutly religious people despise psychics, Magic 8 Balls, fortune-telling, fortune cookies and anything of that ilk, considering them all calling cards of the devil. So I was pretty sure that when I told him about Allison he'd blow up or go into his lecture mode, but he didn't, and yet it was unmistakable that he disapproved. He asked, "Tell me more about the words 'Oh, I say.'"

"It was this character Jason and I had between us."

"And?"

"He was a giraffe. Named Gerard."

"Why did he say, 'Oh, I say'?"

"Because he needed to have a cheesy tag line every time he appeared on our stage, so to speak." It felt uncomfortable, if not obscene, discussing the characters with an outsider. Especially with Reg, who as a child probably spent his Sundays scanning the dot patterns in the weekend funnies with a magnifying glass in search of hidden messages from the devil.

I told Reg about Froggles, too. "Reg, my point is that these were characters shared solely between Jason and *me*. Nobody on the planet could possibly have known about them."

Reg was silent. This drove me nuts. "Reg, say something, at least."

He poured the tea. "I guess what's strange for me here is to learn that Jason had an inner world that included all these characters and all the things they said."

"Well, he *did*."

"And that he spoke with them all the time."

"He didn't speak *with* them, he *was* them. Or rather, they were *us*. We both have our own personalities, but when we went into character mode we became something altogether different. You could give me a thousand bucks and I couldn't think up a single line for them to say. Jason, too. But me and Jason together? There'd be no stopping us."

"Do you have any wine?"

"White or red?"

"White."

I took the bottle out of the fridge and poured it for him. He said, "Ahhh, God bless vitamin W."

I asked him if the psychic aspect of these events upset him for religious reasons.

"Psychics? Lord, no. They're all quacks. I don't believe God speaks to humans through them. So if a psychic's sending you messages, either the psychic's faking it, or something ungodly is coming through."

"Yeah, well . . ."

"Look, Heather, I know you're upset that I don't believe in your psychic."

"She gave me *evidence,* Reg – "

He raised his hands as if to say, *Nothing I can do about it.*

Meanwhile I had to make dinner. I had no idea what was in the fridge to eat – fat-free yogurt? Limp celery? I got up to inspect. I had this thought: "Reg, is all this supposed to make us better people? I mean, is that why we're going through this – so that our souls can somehow improve?" I found a plastic tub of frozen spaghetti sauce.

"Maybe."

I was so mad that I slammed the sauce onto the counter and the lid popped off. "Will you just tell me why it is that the only way we ever seem to take steps forward in life is through pain? Huh? Why is exposure to pain always supposed to make us better people?"

"Heather, it's grotesque to think for even a moment that suffering in and of itself makes you a better person."

"I'm listening."

"Heather, I'm having one of my good days today. I'm not feeling as full of doubt as last time. Doubt comes and goes. And my thinking today is that it's equally grotesque to think that a lack of bad events in your life means you're a good person. Life is only so long. The whistle gets blown, and when it does, where you are is where you are. If people lived to be five hundred, that's probably be about long enough for everybody to have experienced most of what there is, and to have done all of the bad stuff, too. But we check out roughly at seventy-two."

"So?"

"So if we assume that God is just – and I think He is, even after everything that's happened – then justice can still be done. Maybe not here on earth, or in our own lifetimes, but for justice to happen then there has to be something beyond this world. Life on this plane is simply too short for justice."

"Huh."

"Some people even give the impression that they've escaped all the bad stuff, but I don't think anybody does. Not really."

"You don't?"

"No."

"I used to be a really nice person, Reg."

"I can't say that about myself."

"But now something's changed and I'm not a nice person anymore. It happened to me today in the mall's bathroom when I was crying. I stopped being nice."

Reg said, "No, no, that's not true."

In any event, I was heating the spaghetti sauce, and I dropped the subject of psychics, evil, Froggles, and Jason, and spoke about those things that float on the surface, things without roots: current events, TV and movies. The moment Reg left I pounced on the phone and called Allison, but she didn't pick up and there was no machine.

I tried again an hour later. Nothing.

I would have called her every three minutes, but then I realized how uncool it would look if Allison came in, looked at her call screening display, and saw that I'd phoned her seventy-eight times. So instead I phoned her three more times, and just now took a sedative my doctor had given me back when Jason first disappeared, but which I've so far refused to take. I'm going to bed.

Monday night 7:00

Work today was hard, and I screwed up several times. I passed on lunch with Jayne from the court next door, and I bought a tuna salad sandwich and some chocolate milk. It sat beside me untouched on the courtyard steps while I began phoning Allison's number once again. How many times had it been, at that point – ten? But I couldn't help it: her number was the combination to a safe, and I desperately wanted in.

By the end of lunch hour, I felt sick – well, more freaked out than sick. I clocked out and drove home, as if home would afford me any comfort. I phoned Allison twice again and then decided at the last minute to visit Jason's mother at the extended-care facility off Lonsdale. She was awake and for an instant seemed to recognize me, but quickly forgot me again. She kept asking for Joyce, Jason's old dog, but I told her about ten times that because I was allergic to her, Joyce was living with Chris down in Silicon Valley.

Then she asked how Jason was. I said he was fine, and then from the innocent expression on her face I time-traveled just a few months in the past to a world where

Jason was still here. I felt relief that we'd decided to not tell her the news.

Tuesday morning 5:30

Allison won't answer her phone, and I'm ready for murder. For the love of God, *how* many times do I have to dial her? I threw all caution to the wind and put her number on autoredial for the entire evening. Then I went and bought a copy of every local newspaper and checked out all the psychics, looking for her.

I went through the Yellow Pages and the Internet, and still nothing. She must have some sort of business alias. I called all the psychics I could, asking who Allison might be, but nobody knew. Some of them tried reeling me in by fishing for what Allison might have been onto. Scum. But all leads went dead. The nerve of this woman – the *nerve* – she knows darn well what it's like to endure what I've endured, and she doesn't return my call.

I can't sleep. Instead, I just think about *her* more and more, and then I think about Jason, somewhere out there in the afterworld trying to reach me, and instead all he connects with is *Allison* in her teal-colored fleece – pilled fleece, at that – who tells me right out of the gate that she's in the business of being a liar. I walk around the condo, talking aloud, telling Jason that he could come directly to me, instead of wasting his time trying to go through this uncommunicative Allison bitch.

I then felt uncharitable and petty. I thought that maybe if I drank a couple of gallons of water, it'd de-gunk anything in my veins or muscles that might be blocking Jason from reaching me directly. Then I figured I was maybe *too* clear, so I drank a shot of tequila.

Oh, God, I think I'm looped right now – but it was only one tequila shot, and my period was a week ago, so I don't know why I'm so wound up. It's going to be light soon. It'll be a clear, cool day, like summer, but the sun's too low on the horizon.

Seasons have always had a strong effect on me. For example, everyone has a question that assaults them the moment they're awake in the morning – usually it's "Where am I?" or sometimes "What day is it?" I always wake up asking "What season is it?" Not even the day but the *season*. A billion years of evolution summed up in one simple question, all based on the planet's wobble. Oh, but I wish it were spring! And oh – if only I could smell some laurels in the path outside the building! But then, on the other hand, if I'm honest, I have to remember that it takes bodies longer to decompose in fall and winter. Oh, Jason, I'm so sorry, honey, I'm sorry I just thought of you like you were merely biomass like potting soil or manure or mulch. That's obviously not true. I don't know what happened to you, but you're still just Jason. You haven't turned into something else yet.

And Allison, you evil cheesy witch. You won't pick up the phone. How dare you. I'm going to find you. Yes, I'm going to find you.

Tuesday morning 11:00

I'm writing this directly into the courtroom's system. Who cares?

A half-hour ago the unthinkable happened: my cell phone went off in the middle of a cross-examination. Whole years go by without people even noticing we exist. We're not supposed to draw attention to ourselves – and so there I sat looking like a twit to everybody in the room, phone bleeping away. Granted, it was probably the most interesting thing to happen in that courtroom since the double murder trial back in '97, but people are staring at me, willing my cheeks to flush red, trying to make me know that they know about *me*. If you were looking at me as I write this, you'd never know that all I want to do in this world is kidnap Allison and tie her to a rack and demand that she tell me what's going on with Jason.

As I turned off the phone, I checked the call display, and of course it was Allison, finally. It's all I can do right now to not climb the walls with my teeth.

Oh, God. Look at these men. What drudgery are these dirtbags discussing now? They're all crooks. You can't imagine all the mining and real estate and offshore crap that wends through this room. You'd be shocked. They'll bankrupt widows and they'll only get a minimum fine and some golf tips from their lawyers. I bet Allison was married to one of these guys. What was his name? *Glenn*. Uh-huh. Glenn, who probably had a 23 handicap, a cholesterol count of 280, and a handful of semitraceable shell corporations. I've met enough Glenns in my time. Some of them hang around at the end of the day and try to pick me up, which I didn't use to mind because it meant that at least I wasn't invisible. But now? *Glenn*. Now I hate Glenn, because Glenn is connected to Allison, and Allison is a witch.

Oh Lord, when is this morning's session going to end?

And Heather, aren't *you* the one who's up the creek, paddle-free, once they read *this* transcript? Screw it. Nobody ever does.

What has *happened* to me? I've gone crazy. I have. Allison isn't evil. She's just stupid. She probably forgot to recharge her phone. Why all of a sudden do you accuse her of treachery when stupidity may be her only failing? Wait a second – Allison is *way* too young a name for a woman aged sixty-ish. She ought to be called Margaret or Judy or Pam. *Allison?* Only women my age are called Allison. Or Heather. When we all start dying in another forty years, they'll look at the obituaries, see our names and say to themselves, "Isn't it weird? All the Heathers are dying."

A bit later

Okay, there was one time when I suspected something dodgy with Jason, just one time, down in Park Royal maybe two months before he disappeared. We were walking down the main atrium in the south mall, returning a shirt, and in mid-conversation Jason froze. I looked at whatever it was he was seeing; there was just this guy sitting there eating ice cream on a bench with a woman who looked to be his mother. He was a big guy, kind of Eastern European looking, and his clothes – they were like what a nightclub bouncer in Vlad-ivostok might choose, thinking that this was how hip Americans dress. His mother was like something from the tuberculosis ward on Ellis Island circa 1902.

"Jason?"

"Don't move."

"Huh."

"I said, don't – "

"Jason, you're scaring me."

The guy looked our way, and in slow motion put down his ice cream. He then rolled up his pants leg, and I thought he was going to pull out a handgun, but instead I saw that he had a metal prosthesis. The guy knocked on it, looked up at Jason and gave a creepy smile.

The next minute Jason had whisked me away and we were standing in front of the Bootlegger jeans store. He was obviously stressed out, and when he saw that we were in front of the Bootlegger store, he became even more so – he said, "Not *this* place." So we escalatored up to the next level. I looked down, and the one-legged guy was looking up at us.

By then I was curious but also quite angry. "Jason, what was *that* all about?"

"A guy I used to work with."

"It doesn't look to me like you were friends with him."

"He burnt me on some money he owes me. He's a crazy Russian guy. Those people will do anything."

"That's racist."

"Whatever. That guy is bad news."

I saw the wall slam down. I didn't bother pursuing the question, as past experience had taught me the futility of trying to breach the wall.

Jason said, "Let's go to the parkade."

"What? We just got here. We haven't even returned this shirt."

"We're going."

And so we left.

And for the weeks after that, Jason was jumpy and tossed in his sleep. Maybe there was no connection to the disappearance. What am I saying? I don't have a clue. But if I ever see that guy again, he's got a lot of questions coming his way.

Tuesday afternoon 1:30

Back in my little stenography booth looking, to all the world, like the picture of industry.

I listened to Allison's message over lunch hour:

"Oh, hello, uh, Heather, this is Allison. I think you might have been trying to reach me. I couldn't find your number because it was in the cell phone's memory and the phone was in the car, which died, and so I've been trying to rustle up some money to get the starter motor fixed, and, well, you know how complicated things can get . . ."

Do I? Do I? Allison, stop feebly toying with the trivialities of your life, accomplishing nothing, pretending that your tasks are so complex that only God could handle them. Just go fix your effing car, and shut up. And yes, Allison, I *do* know how complicated things can get, but they could be bloody well easier if you'd stop pretending to be a cretinous fake helpless girly-girl about matters that take only ten minutes to solve.

". . . Anyway, yes, I did have a remarkable statement for you come through last night, and it was for you, no mistake there. Would you like to get together maybe at the end of the day? I know you work nine to five. Here's my number, give me a call . . ."

Hag.

As if I didn't know her number. I phoned it and got no response. Lunch hour went by in what seemed to be three minutes as I dialed it over and over, for a few minutes from the bathroom because I got a bit dizzy and had to sit in silence. What is it about Allison that has me sitting in public bathroom stalls all the time?

So now I'm back in the courtroom supposedly documenting this frivolous and endless land deal trial. These men should all be tarred and feathered and be flogged as they walk naked down the street for screwing around with the lives of common people the way they do.

In my peripheral vision I'm also noticing that people are looking at me to see if my cell phone is going to ring again. As if. But I have to admit, it's a bit flattering to be the temporary star in the courtroom, instead of these blowhards who drag things out so they can bill for countless hours. The law is a lie. It's a lie. A lie.

Tuesday afternoon 2:45

Back in my little booth stenographing away.

My phone just rang again. Right in the middle of a freighted moment engineered by one of these hawklike balding Glennoids. The judge spoke to me quite harshly – too harshly, really; I mean, it's only a cell phone ringing in front of the court. Professionally it's a huge humiliation, but you know what? I could care less. I told his honor that I'd just signed up for a new cell phone program and that I was unfamiliar with their system. And he bought it.

And so here I am, chastened, and to look at me, I'm beavering away at my job, humiliated and belittled by the powers above. Sure. I just want to get out of this psychic garbage dump.

Tuesday night 10:00

Allison finally answered her phone. I pretended to be all-innocent, as if I hadn't phoned her two thousand times in the past forty-eight hours.

"Allison?"

"Heather. We connect. How are you?"

Like a Ryder truck full of fertilizer and diesel fuel, with a detonator set at thirty seconds and ticking. "Okay. Getting by. The usual. You?"

"Oh, you know – this car of mine. Cars are so expensive to maintain."

"What do you drive?"

"A '92 Cutlass."

Well, of course it's expensive to maintain. It's a decade old – what do you expect? The quality revolution hadn't happened then. It's one big hunk of pain you're driving. Throw it away. Buy a Pontiac Firefly for $19.95 – I don't care what you do, but for God's sake, don't drive the wind-up toy you're using now. I said, "Cars are getting better these days, but they can still be a bother."

"The money I make from being a pretend psychic is so small."

"I could help you out, maybe."

"*Could* you?"

I said, "Sure. It's probably going to cost less than you thought. I can set you up with my repair guy, Gary, down on Pemberton Avenue."

"That'd be kind of you."

"So can we meet tonight?"

"I think so."

I asked, "What time works for you?"

"Seven o'clock"?

"Where? How about my place?"

"Oh . . ."

"Allison – is everything okay?"

"It's just that seven is when I usually eat dinner."

We agreed to meet at a slightly formal Italian place on Marine Drive. When I arrived, it was evident she'd been there a while, as only the dregs remained in what I already saw was a bottle of the restaurant's priciest merlot. She told me I looked relaxed, which is always a successful ploy, because it invariably relaxes the person you say it to. I asked if she liked the wine; she did – she'd better – and she ordered another bottle, although you'd never imagine such a tiny dragon could hold her booze so well.

Heather, try to be nice to this woman. You're only jealous because Jason chose to speak through her and not directly to you.

As soon as there was wine in my glass I asked her what message Jason had given her, but she raised her hand in a warding-off motion (very professional) and said, "It's not good to mix eating with the spirit world." It was all I could do not to throttle her. She talks about the afterlife like it was Fort Lauderdale.

As Allison didn't want to contaminate her perceptions by asking me about my life, I learned – over the appetizer, the lamb entrée, and some Key lime sorbet – about Glenn, who had worked for the Port Authority's inspection division, further details of which make me ache for sleep. She has three ungrateful daughters, all in their twenties, who seem to shack up with anything on two legs. To hear Allison's side of the story, her life has been nothing but person after person abusing her sweet, generous nature. Of course, I don't believe her for a moment, but that doesn't get me anywhere. She's got the sole existing phone line to Jason, and I'll be damned if some passive-aggressive menopausal old bat is going to cheat me out of hearing what Jason's been saying to me.

When the dishes were cleared, Allison did what I used to do back in college, which was keep a sharp eye attuned to the restaurant's till so as to see when the check might be arriving, and once the check was in motion toward the table, flee to the bathroom. When she returned, she found me putting on my sweater and readying my purse.

"Oh, did the bill come?"

"My treat."

"How sweet of you."

"Maybe we could go to a coffee place and discuss, you know – these things you've been receiving."

"That's an excellent idea."

We found a nearby café inhabited by local teens primping and strutting and turkey-cocking, all of which made me feel older than dirt. Allison ordered the most expensive coffee on the menu, whereupon I gave her my most penetrating stare. "Can we talk now about Jason?"

"Of course, dear. But I wish it didn't feel as silly as it does to say these things to you."

"No, not at all. So what did he say?"

Allison inhaled and delivered the words like an embarrassing truth. "Glue."

"What?"

"Glue. Glue glue glue glue glue."

I was floored. It was the Quails speaking. The Quails were

yet more characters created by Jason and me – a blend of Broadway gypsies and intelligent children, greatly given to repetitive tasks and themed costumes. But the Quails spoke only their own language, which had only one word, *glü,* with a jaunty, Ikea-like umlaut on the ü.

Allison said, "After all your kindness, Heather, that's the only message I have for you. I think maybe I am a fraud after all."

I sat stunned.

"Heather? Heather?"

"What? I – "

"I take it this means something to you."

"Yeah. It does."

"That's a relief."

Allison, I suppose, was wondering what kind of genie had been let out of the bottle. I asked her, "Nothing else? Nothing at all?"

"Sorry Heather. Just *'Glue glue glue glue.'* "

"When do you normally pick up your messages, so to speak?"

"It has to be during the night."

"So tonight you'll get more?"

"I can only wait and see."

"Will you call me if you get anything?"

"Of course I will. But I think it's because of my car and money worries that I'm blocking more than I could otherwise receive."

"I'll help you out with your car. And of course I'll pay you your normal psychic fees."

"You're very kind, Heather. And after tonight's lavish meal, too."

Oh, brother. I took ten twenty-dollar bills from my bag and gave them to Allison. "This is for today. And also, I'll cover your car's repair bill this time. How does that sound?"

"Such kindness! But really Heather, you – "

I was swept away in the emotion of hearing Quails from the dead. "It's my pleasure. Can I ask you to keep your phone on tomorrow, Allison? It's so frustrating to be unable to reach you sometimes."

"Of course I will, dear."

And so I came home, where I'm sitting now trying to make sense of Jason's happy message from beyond. *Glü glü glü glü glü glü glü glü glü glü glü glü glü.*

I'm wondering if I should just jump off Cleveland Dam and get to him right away, but that would probably somehow disqualify me.

So I think I just need to sit here, enjoy the glow and then take two sleeping pills because tomorrow's a working day.

Just before I fall asleep . . .

I've been thinking. I'm older. I'm on the other side of thirty-five, and I have a better notion of wasted time and energy than I did even two years ago. If somebody wastes my time these days, I get mad. I'm also seven years older than Jason, but after about thirty-three, we're all the same age in our heads, so it's not the big deal it looks like. At least not from the inside looking out. And as Jason was almost thirty-three, we were almost the same. And anyway, a few decades after your first kiss and your first cigarette, I don't care if you're rich or poor, life leaves the same number of bruises on you.

Most people might view Jason as a failure, and that's just

fine. Failure is authentic, and because it's authentic, it's real and genuine, and because of that, it's a pure state of being. I thought Jason was as pure and bright as a halo, and no, I'm not trying to make excuses for the guy. God only knows he snored through enough morning jobs, and he clocked out early once a week to watch the games down at the pubs. But Jason never curried favor with people he didn't like. He never tried to fake being busy so he'd look good, and he never fudged his opinion to suit the temperature of the room.

In failure, Jason could be truly himself, and there's a liberation that stems from that. Leave that shirt untucked. Wash your hair tomorrow. Beer with lunch? Sure.

I wish I could say that success turns people into plastic dolls, but the truth is that I don't know any successful people. The people in the courts are the closest I might come to knowing success stories, but they're all vermin.

At first I wondered if I should take Jason and clean him up and turn him into a gung-ho PowerPoint-driven success story, but that was never going to happen. I figured that out quickly, so I never pushed him. That I didn't try to force him to change might have been my biggest attraction – that and my manicotti Florentine – and the fact that I never judged him harshly, or even judged him at all. I simply let him be who he was, this sweet, screwed-up refugee from a past that was so extreme and harsh, and so different from my own. And he was so lonely when I met him – oh! He almost hummed with relief in the mornings when he learned we could talk at breakfast. Apparently, that was forbidden growing up. Reg must have been pretty gruesome back then.

Jason also had this thing called the glory-meter. A glory-meter was an invisible device Jason said almost everybody carries around with them, a Palm Pilot–ish gadget that goes *ding-ding-ding* whenever we come up with a salve to try to inflate our sense of importance. Examples would be "I make the best sour cherry pie in Vancouver"; "My dachshund has the silkiest fur of all the dogs in the park"; "My spreadsheets have the most sensibly ordered fields"; "I won the 500-yard dash in my senior year." You get the picture. Simple stuff. Jason never saw anything wrong with this kind of thing, but when he pointed the meter to himself, the *ding-ding-ding* stopped, and he'd pretend to whack it, as if the needle were broken.

"Jason, you must have *something* in you to activate the glory-meter."

"Sorry, honey. Nada."

"Oh, come on . . ."

"Zilch."

This was his cue for me to say how much I loved him, and I'd spend the next ten minutes girlishly telling him all the goofy things I like about him, and he felt so much better because of that. So, if that's fixing someone, yup, I fixed the man.

Wednesday morning 10:30

I ended up needing five sleeping pills to knock me out, and it was all I could do to drag my butt into work this morning. As an antidote, I took some trucker pills Jason kept in the medicine cabinet – heavy duty, but they do wake me up. Fortunately, people will misinterpret my sour, inwardly turned face as contrition after yesterday's cell phone debacle. However, I can barely think properly, let alone transcribe the boring pap being spouted in this current trial, so I'm just going to sit here and do the best I can, given the circumstances.

Oh, it's lovely to sit here and pay no attention to anything these morons in the court are saying. I ought to have tried this years ago. I wonder how many other stenographers across the decades have sat here pumping out their inner self while appearing prim and methodical? Oh, I suppose I'm flattering myself, but we're a good crew, we are, stenographers. On TV, we never get to be a part of the plot twist. A star has never played a stenographer; there isn't even a porn movie with court stenographers in it.

Right now, a lawyer named Pete is prattling on about a property conveyance form that's not been supplied. I smell a recess coming up.

I suppose I can phone Allison during the recess. I thought about her way too much last night. There's something I don't like about her, but what could be her angle? So far she's gotten a good meal, maybe some free car repairs and two hundred bucks from me. Not much.

Who am I fooling? This woman *owns* me. And she knows it. And I can only pray that I get enough messages from Jason before she bares her fangs and starts upping the price.

Heather, get a grip: she's a North Vancouver widow – which is pretty much what you are, too – a widow who's trying to scam some bucks and hold onto a middle-class façade before poverty sucks her down the drain like some cheap special effect.

Are Allison's actions criminal? One fact I know from being a stenographer is that just about anybody can do just about anything for just about any reason. Crime is what got me into stenography. I wanted to see the faces of people who lie. I wanted to see how people can say one thing and do another. It's all my parents ever did with each other, as well as with all their family members. I thought being closer to liars and criminals could help me put my family's lies into better perspective – but of course that never happened. At least I sometimes had entertainment. Like a few years ago we had this woman, an elementary school teacher, who claimed she was at a baby shower when it turns out she was quite happily dismembering her father-in-law. I wanted to see that kind of lying brio. She maintained total composure while the defense team clobbered her with motive – money, what else? – and intent – she'd bought a kiddy pool a month earlier in order to contain the blood – plus there were receipts for hundreds of dollars' worth of bleach and disinfectants and deodorants, purchased from the same Shoppers Drug Mart where I buy my tampons and microwave popcorn.

Was there a big moral to any of this? Doubtful. But I do know that as a species we're somehow hard-wired to believe lies. It's astonishing how willing we are to believe whatever story we're tossed simply because we want to hear what we want to hear.

I suppose I also thought that being a stenographer hearing it all would somehow inoculate me against crimes occurring *to* me. Naïve. But then, it was a seventeen-year-old me who made that decision. Imagine leaving your most important life decisions to a seventeen-year-old! What was God thinking? If there's such a thing as reincarnation, I want the nature of my next incarnation to be decided by a quorum of twelve seventysomethings.

What's this? Goody gumdrops – a recess while Joe Dirtbag buys time to find a conveyance form that every person in the courtroom knows doesn't exist. Rich people have their own laws; poor people don't stand a chance; they never have.

Tuesday afternoon 3:00

I was eating lunch in a café near the courthouse, picking at some romaine lettuce leaves while dispiritedly redialing Allison, when some French Canadian girls behind me, tree planters – teenagers with perfect skin and no apparent sense of gratitude for what society has given them – began discussing vegetarianism and meat. Their descriptions of Quebec slaughterhouses were so foul that I almost vomited, though normally such explicit dialogue would only leave me curious for more. I stumbled back to the courthouse, found Larry who does shift planning and pleaded off sick for the remainder of the day – again. I drove home, where all I could do was lie beneath the duvet and think about where Jason's body is right now. Not his soul or spirit, but the *meat* part of him. Why is this so important to me?

I know he was no prince before I met him; as I've said, that was part of the attraction. As well, my chosen vocation prepares a person for the worst of what can happen to the human body, coroner's photos included, even in happy little Vancouver: bride burnings, and women tossed into wood chippers, then sent to the rendering plant.

God knows Jason had some gruesome images locked up inside him. After I met him, I called in a favor from Lori, who works in the archives. I asked her to pull photo files for me on the Delbrook Massacre – the photos from the cafeteria. Well, all I can say is that the media does both a service and a disservice by not showing the real story there. I suppose there are Web sites where you can go look at this kind of stuff, but . . .

Okay, the fourth photo down was of Cheryl.

I stopped breathing when I saw her.

Her.

So *young*. Oh, dear God, so young. All of them. Just babies. And Cheryl's face was unspeckled by any gore, despite the battlefield around her. In the photo she looked serene, as if she were alive and suntanning. There was no fear there. None.

I put the photos back in the envelope; I didn't look at the rest.

Would Jason feel better if he knew that she'd died at peace? But he must have known this. If he returned, would I tell him I'd seen the photo? Would that drive him away or bond us closer?

If he returned.

Bastard.

Why couldn't he have left me a clue? A simple measly clue. But no: "Just going out to get some smokes, honey. Want anything? Milk? Bananas?" He's dead. He has to be. Because he'd never simply leave me. He wasn't like that.

I keep on wondering which of his friends might have had some inkling of what was going on, but Jason was, aside from me, alone in the world. His family was one notch less than totally useless. I get so mad at them sometimes. I mean, his mother dragged him off to hillbilly country the moment the massacre investigation cleared him; he never properly faced his accusers, and they must have felt they'd somehow won something in that.

Kent was dead, but he could have stuck up for his little brother instead of hiding behind a wall of midterms and religious hocus-pocus.

And there's Reg – Reg, why did you have to wait for the world to collapse around you before you became a human being? You two would have gotten along so well, you really would have.

And don't even get me going about Cheryl's plastic, mean-spirited parents. Hypocrites.

Even Barb gets a bit clippy when I talk about Jason too much.

Egad – I'm just venting here. It's merely me venting. These are all kind people. And I'm merely venting.

And I also can't get Cheryl's photo out of my head. I'm not the jealous type, but when it comes to her, what's a girl supposed to do? In the eyes of the world, Cheryl's a saint. Who else on earth has a saint for competition – nuns?

But I don't think she was a saint – not judging by what I could learn from Jason. I think she was just an average girl who was maybe missing a sense of drama in her life. Since Jason's disappearance, I've had dinner a few times with Chris and Cheryl's parents over at Barb's; all they talk about is getting deals on cases of canned corn at Costco, the best price they got on Alaska Airlines tickets to Scottsdale, and the new next-door neighbors who don't use English as a first language. I've never heard them discuss an idea at the table, let alone give much thought to where Jason might be. My presence there possibly unnerves them. Jason said that they were vile and that they still suspected him of being the one who videotaped the gunmen and mailed the tapes to the press, but I didn't get any inkling of that from them. If anything, I sensed regret that they'd never gotten to really meet him.

As for Cheryl, I quickly learned that she could pop up anywhere. We'd be watching TV and *blink* there she was, her yearbook photo on the screen and a voice-over talking about crime and youth, or spiraling crime rates or crime and women. This was always jarring for me, but never for Jason. He'd smile slightly and say, "Don't worry." But you know, I saw his face. He was still in love with her. It's there.

What's bizarre is that I (being alive) have the competitive edge over her (being dead). Yet at the same time she (being dead) has the edge over me (alive but aging quickly, and not very well at that).

And then there's religion. Even though Jason said he'd shunned religion, I have this feeling that life, for him, was just a waiting game, and that he believed if he could squeak through the rest of his life, he'd meet up with Cheryl. How do I know that his disdain for religion wasn't short-term? I tried talking to Jason about Cheryl, but his answers were politician's answers: "She was someone in my life so long ago. I was a kid." But she died in his arms in a lake of blood!

Jason also said a few things over the years to make me wonder if the tree, having been chopped down to the ground, was now sending new shoots out from the soil. For example, we saw a childhood friend of his, Craig, on the highway driving a Ferrari or one of those cars. Jason said, "Well you know, you can accumulate all the stuff you want in this life, but stuff alone can't make you happy. Craig there has to go around acting like he's a complete man, now. Right."

"You're just jealous."

"No, I'm not."

And he wasn't.

Reg hasn't tried to convert me in the past months, nor even edge in that direction. He's far too preoccupied with the state of his own soul. Ironically, his honesty about his doubts has made him genuinely spiritual and has made me far more open to his ideas than I might have been otherwise. I don't think Reg has realized this. When I'm around him, I find myself cross-examining my motives for everything I do. I think I'm a moral person, yet I'm always wondering if there's the ghost of Cheryl out there, watching me, saying, "Look out, Heather, don't confuse your morality with God's demands."

So it all comes back to Cheryl and my (let's face it) jealousy. Here's what I think: the five most unattractive traits in people are cheapness, clinginess, neediness, unwillingness to change and jealousy. Jealousy is the worst, and by far the hardest to conceal. Around Jason I made myself conceal it, because what else could I do? But I don't know how to kill jealousy. I fully expect it to turn into little steel fangs that'll clutch me like a leghold trap the moment I need to be most tender or forgiving. Jealousy is the one emotion that *lies in wait*.

Thursday morning 6:00

No sleeping pills last night, and Allison has revealed the full length of her fangs. First, a call came in from my car guy down on Pemberton: "Hi, Heather, it's Gary."

"Gary, hi."

"Heather, I've got some lady came in here, jittery old

thing, like a librarian with the clap – got a whole bunch of repairs done on this old boat of a Cutlass, and then she says you're the one who's supposed to be paying for all of it. I'm in the back room right now, and I just have to ask you if this is the case or what."

"How much, Gary?"

"With taxes, just over two grand."

"Holy – "

"That's what I thought."

I paused before saying, "Gary, I'll pay."

"You sure about that, Heather?"

"Yeah, I'm sure."

I put down the phone and tried to appraise my new situation coolly. I was her slave. Trust me, having one's paranoia confirmed can be a relaxing, almost sedative sensation.

The first thing I did was stop phoning her. I knew she'd phone me, and she'd only do so when she knew the time was right to strike. This freed me to do things I'd been neglecting. I cleaned up the place, as though performing an FBI crime scene sweep: I put everything of Jason's that held his smell in extra-large Ziploc freezer bags. All his toiletries – his razors, his brushes: *bagged*. His wallet by the fruit bowl: *bagged*. I bagged his dirty underwear and T-shirts and shoes. I also bagged all the clothing that was in his hamper. Once I'd isolated all his personal effects, I opened each bag and held it up to my face and inhaled for all I was worth. I wondered how much longer his odor would last. The smell of his cheap underarm deodorant made me cry. I drank most of a bottle of Bailey's and passed out – much better than sleeping pills. I was woken up around nine this morning by a phone call from Larry, asking if I was okay. I said I was sick. I *am* sick.

I looked at the pile of Jason's things. I knew I had to start my life all over again from scratch. I could go to work, sure, but I'd be a husk. There was no way I'd ever meet anybody again, and in real life I'd become the invisible blank of a person I pretended to be in the courtroom.

So where do you start when you want to start your life again? At least when you're young you're also stupid. But me? *Tick tick tick.*

I made coffee and was going to call Barb when the phone rang.

"Hello?"

"Hello, Heather. It's Allison."

"Hello, Allison." My voice was stripped of spark, a prisoner's voice.

"I thought I'd call. See how you're doing. I had another message come to me."

"You did, did you?"

"Yes. And it was quite a long one."

"That's nice."

"Should we get together?"

"Yes, Allison, we ought to get together. Why don't I come to your office or wherever it is you work."

"I work from home."

"Why don't I come to your house?"

"Oh, no – I never let clients come here."

"How much is your rate for the session going to be, Allison?"

This was the clincher.

"Allison?"

"Five thousand dollars."

"I figured as much."

"So then where do you think we should meet?"

I knew that someplace private where I could wallop the crap out of her wasn't an option, so I suggested a restaurant at Park Royal that catered mostly to older diners who liked buttery European food. She seemed to like this.

"Oh, and Heather – "

"Yes, Allison?"

"Cash, please."

At one in the afternoon I met her there. It was odd pretending to be civil when she was in the midst of vile extortion. Allison said, "All this butter and oil – you'd think pensioners would take better care of their hearts."

"They're just waiting to die, Allison. Give it a rest."

Wiener schnitzels appeared on the table, but I didn't touch mine; Allison's vanished as though eaten by a cartoon wolf. As she downed her last bite, she said, "There. Now shall we get down to business?"

"Yes, Allison, let's."

"Do you have the payment?"

I showed her the money, in twenties, taken from the shared account Jason and I were using to save for a down payment on a small house. It was inside one of the leftover Ziploc bags. "Here."

She appraised it quickly. "Fine. I had a message last night. I don't known what any of this means, but here goes . . ." She then began mouthing the words she'd received. It was one of our favorite set pieces, involving Henry Chickadee, "Heir to the Chickadee Seed Fortune." Henry's story is that he spent his days in Aisle 17 of the local Wal-Mart saying,

"Hello! Welcome to Aisle 17. I'm Henry Chickadee, might I entice you to sample our wide variety of Chickadee Seed products?" Sometimes Henry would be in his perch beside a small mirror, and when he went back and forth on his swing, he'd say "Hello!" every time he saw himself. Henry didn't understand what mirrors were, or what they did, and if other characters tried to explain it, he'd just gap out. Pure silliness.

And so Allison sat there, in the middle of this geriatric restaurant reeking of buttery foods, saying *"Hello! Hello! Hello."* Even though this woman was evil, she delivered the goods.

"Was there anything else added on to that?"

"Well – "

"Yes?" Fleeced or not, I was starved for connection.

"He says he misses you. He says he feels lost without you. He says he tries to speak to you, but he can't. He apologizes for having to speak through me."

My eyes were watering. I'd gotten what I wanted. Allison said to me, "I apologize for being hard to reach, but I have to do what I can to protect my channel into the afterworld."

"Yeah. Sure. Whatever."

"I'll be phoning you soon."

"I'm sure you will."

I didn't say thank you, and she didn't seem to expect it. She and her depressing pilled teal-fleece jacket left the restaurant. I threw some bills onto the table and followed her down the mall and out into the parking lot, where she got into her claptrap Cutlass. I took her license number, went home and called Lori, my mole. She gave me the name and address of one Cecilia Bateman, at an address in Lynn

Valley, a 1960s subdivision that had been missed by every scourge of redevelopment since. I waited until dark and I went there. I parked a few houses down from Allison's, on one of the neighborhood's steeply sloping streets. The darkened trees, in silhouette, seemed as deep as lakes. Maybe at some point in its past, this neighborhood was sunny and scraped clean, but now it was a place where you could torture hitchhikers in complete freedom, the loudest of screams never getting past the rhododendron borders. I felt like I was fifteen again, spying with my old friend Kathy on the Farrells who, as teen legend had it, were highly sexed and given to orgies. The most we ever saw was handsome Mr. Farrell in his Y-fronts sucking beer and watching hockey, but to this day, Y-fronts get me going pretty quickly.

But back to Allison . . .

Or rather, back to *Cecilia*.

I walked up a driveway so steep as to feel dreamlike. From a real estate agent's point of view, chez Cecilia was a tear-down, but so is most of North and West Vancouver. This kind of 1963 house was so familiar to me that I didn't pause to acknowledge its ludicrous existence, at the top of a mountain where nobody should ever live, a yodel away from pristine wilderness, an existence made possible only through petroleum and some sort of human need for remaining remote while being relatively close to many others. Even in the dark, I could see that the house was stained a sun-drained blue, like bread mold, the same color as this Allison/Cecilia woman's car.

So yes, I saw her car in the garage – one car only. There were a number of lights on, and I could hear the dull glugging sounds of a TV in the background. I went through the garage, around to the back of the house. Nothing had been mowed in years, and my clothes were a magnet for leaves and cedar droppings and cobwebs.

Why was I even here? I didn't want to murder her, even though it would have been fairly easy to do so. I didn't want to confront her, because I didn't want to lose my connection to Jason. Cecilia's the only game in town.

I maneuvered closer to the back of the house and looked in the windows with impunity; there she was, rooting around in the freezer, removing a cardboard box containing a TV dinner. She put it on a butcher-block counter and removed the cardboard top. She read the French-language end of the carton, turned it around to the English end, then proceeded to timidly poke one, two, three holes in the dinner tray's plastic film. She opened her microwave's door, put the meal inside, punched some buttons and then – and then she just stood there for maybe three minutes, her arms across her chest, contemplating her existence. This is when I felt the chill. This is when I once more realized that Allison/Cecilia is basically me – an older version of me, but a woman marooned, manless and geographically remote, contemplating a life of iffy labor, a few thousand more microwaveable meals and then a coffin.

She had just removed her meal from the microwave when I heard a noise down in the carport, as did Allison. I could see headlights through the branches of various species of evergreen; Allison dropped (rather than put) her meal on the counter, reached into a drawer, found an amber-brown prescription container and removed one or more pills, which she swallowed without water. The headlights went out; I heard a door slam, and then watched as Allison stood in the

210

center of her kitchen, the plastic membrane not yet removed from her meal's surface.

A youngish woman entered. Twenty-five? I couldn't make out what they were saying, but from my disastrous relationship with my own mother, the bingo zombie, I could tell that this young woman was Cecilia's daughter and that hurtful words were being hurled back and forth. God, how nice to be on the sidelines for this, and to not be the one hurling.

For a moment, my sympathies were with Allison, until I remembered that she was out to hose-clean my bank account while pinballing my emotions to the max.

In any event, they went off into the living room, which was on the second floor, up front, not visible from anywhere I could position myself. I circled the house a few times, decided it was time to quit the stalking and skulked down the driveway to my car. I forgot to brush all of the dead leaves and insects and webs from my outfit first, and discovered a spider crawling across my chest. I had a freakout, madly swiped the thing away from me, and when I got back in the car I was breathing like a dying coal miner as the car door's alarm went *ding-ding-ding-ding-ding*.

From there I drove to Reg's apartment. Reg was obviously surprised when I buzzed his intercom, but he said come on in. The building's lobby smelled of disinfectant, cooking and dust. The elevator dropped me off on the eighteenth floor, into a muggy, airless little hallway. Jason had once told me how claustrophobic and killingly dark Reg's place was, but it's hard to imagine it being as bad as all that. He was standing at the opened door. "Heather?"

Of course I blubbered, and Reg motioned me into his apartment. Even through the tears and the emotional funk, I could see it was not at all the way Jason had described it. I guess it was Scandinavian modern, interior decor not being something I usually notice. Reg could see my surprise above and beyond what was already on my face: "Ruth made me sell everything years ago. Jason told you it was a mausoleum in here, didn't he?"

I nodded.

"Well, it was. I think most of this stuff came from Dirndl or whatever those places are called. I kind of like it – the removal of excess things from our lives is always a blessing. Let me get you a drink."

"Water."

"Water then."

He brought back a glass of water, a bottle of white wine and some glasses. "Tell me what happened."

"It was *her*."

"I guessed as much. Go on."

"She's robbing me blind."

"How?"

"She's charging me five thousand bucks a message now."

Reg said nothing.

"And I'm *paying* it. She knows things that only ever went as far as our pillows. In tiny detail – things you couldn't guess at even if you knew Jason and me our entire lives."

"Go on."

"So I went to her house."

Reg flinched: "You didn't do anything rash, did you?"

"*No*. Nothing at all. She's a North Van widow living in a junker of a house in Lynn Valley . . . and she *owns* me."

"Have some wine. Calm down a minute."

He was right: I needed to level out, return to my normal

stenographical demeanor so I could at least find some detachment. He changed the subject and we talked about small things, but I must have resembled a troll doll, covered with yard lint, my mascara running. A few minutes later he brought me a hot washcloth and a clothes brush; I scrubbed clean my face and removed the spiderwebs from my sweater. Reg then started the train of thought that has me here at four in the morning typing away.

"Look, Heather," he asked, "have you considered all the angles on this?"

"Of course I have."

"No, really, have you?"

"Reg, you're implying something, but I don't know what."

"Heather, you're the only person I can talk to anymore. Everyone else is either gone or they've crossed me off their list."

"That's not true. Barb still talks to – "

"Yes, I know, Barb still talks to me, but only out of duty and, I'm guessing, loyalty to you."

"What are you telling me?"

"I'm telling you that I don't believe in psychics. I'm telling you that I don't think the dead can talk to us in any way. Once you're there, you're there. I doubt Jason's been kid-napped and is being held hostage, but at the same time I can't help but wonder what some other genuine reason for this might be."

"How could Allison have known such intimate – ?"

"The point is, Allison – or Cecilia or whatever her name is – doesn't speak with the dead. There is a link between her and Jason."

I was speechless.

"I'm not saying they had an affair. Or anything like that."

"The daughter."

"What?"

"The daughter. That's who I saw coming in the garage."

"How do you know it's her daughter? Heather?"

It made perfect sense. *Heather, you freaking idiot.* "Allison has never had a signal in her life. It's her daughter – Jason was using our characters with someone else. *Her.*"

"That's jumping to conclusions."

"Is it?"

"I think it is. Jason loved you. He'd never have . . ."

I jumped up and told Reg I had to go. He said, "Heather, don't go. Not now. You're crazy right now. Oh dear God, stop where you are."

But Reg couldn't change my mind, and I went right out the door and drove, slightly drunk, to Allison's house. And that's where I am now, parked, typing into my laptop, waiting, waiting, waiting for the lights to go on inside, watching those two cars in the carport. I can wait here all night. I can wait here forever.

It's getting so hard to remember who Jason was, that he had a voice, that he had his own way of speaking and of seeing the world. He's like a character in a book, trying to make sense of the world as it played out for him. My own book is just one more tossed onto the heap. How did he speak? How did he smile? I have photos. I have videos of barbecues with him at Barb's, and a few risqué tapes of us together, which I had the wit not to throw away. But I'm too frightened to watch because they're *the end*. After them there's nothing. His smells are in the little bags, decaying.

What am I to do? Jason was an accident. No – Jason was God coming down and tampering with the laws of nature to effect a miracle in my life. People are hung up on miracles, but miracles are called miracles because they pretty much never happen. So then, *who* put that dorky little giraffe wearing the suspiciously manly sheepskin jacket on the counter at Toys R Us that afternoon? I was his witness. I made him real, and he made *me* real. I remember being single for so very long – I remember making mental lists of compromises I was willing to make in order to get me to 76.5 years without snapping. *If I only go to see two movies a week, one by myself, one with a friend, that'll make two nights of the week pass without quaking. Don't phone my friends in relationships too often or I'll look too desperate. Don't become godmother to too many of my friends' children or else I'll become a maiden-aunt punch line. Don't drink more than three drinks a night ever because I like drinking, and it could easily plaster over all of my cracks.*

When I was eleven I broke my arm investigating a new house being built in our family's subdivision. It spent the summer in a cast, like an itching, tormenting worm burning with pink fiberglass strands, and I thought the weeks would never pass – but then they did, and I remember forgetting about that cast not even six hours after having it removed (Oh, the cool air!) And so it was with Jason.

Once he entered my life, I promptly forgot all my years of putting on a brave face while browsing at bookstores until closing time, and of having one, two, three beers while watching crime shows and CNN. I completely forgot the hateful sensation of loneliness, like thirst and hunger together pressing on my stomach.

A few times my old single friends came over to eat with Jason and me at our dumpy but happy little place, and I could tell that they were planning to politely remove themselves from my life. All those great women who went with me to Mel Gibson movies and two-for-one Caesar night at the Keg – I trashed them out of my life. And I could see the fear in their eyes as they realized that they were, each of them, just one more notch alone in the world. Sometimes my lonely single friends would wait until Jason was out and then they'd come visit me, sitting and ranting for hours about how brilliant they were, and yet the world was screwing them over, and the core of their being was hollowing as a result. I was prideful – I was glad I wasn't lonely. I wanted to insulate myself from lonely people and, to be honest, so many other forms of human suffering.

Heather, you bitch, betraying your friends for some man.

Jason! You're not just some man. You're my only guy, but you're fading on me, like a waning crescent moon going behind Bowen Island around sunset. The next day you may well be there, but I won't be seeing you.

Monday (four days later)

And so here I am at work in court. I'll be quitting this afternoon. I told Larry I'd fill in just this one shift and then I'm gone. God only knows who'll ever read these words. Here's what happened:

I was in the car outside Allison's, nodding off around 8:30 in the morning, when I saw the daughter pull out of the driveway in a red Ford Escort like every other car on earth. In a spasm of efficiency I got my car revved and I trailed her down Mountain Highway, then over the Second Narrows Bridge, where she pulled onto Commissioner Street, which follows the canning factories and docks as they approach downtown: wheat-choked CN trains covered in graffiti, with haloes of pigeons; plastic tubs full of fish offal, scuffed and bloody; forklifts; concrete mixers. Mount Baker was like the Paramount logo in the south toward the U.S., and the gulls and geese were seemingly dancing in the flawless blue sky for my enjoyment. It was a cold, clear October day. I don't think I ever remember feeling quite so alert as I did following Allison's daughter.

The harbor was flat as a cookie sheet, and I had a déjà vu that went on for almost half an hour. Usually a déjà vu, like happiness, vanishes the moment you recognize it, but not during that particular drive. And I didn't feel alone. Someone was in my car with me – a ghost? Who knows? Funny, but whoever it was, it wasn't Jason. It was – oh, hooey. I don't go in for that stuff anymore. Not after what happened.

Okay then, what *did* happen?

I followed the daughter's car into the small parking lot behind a company that sold marine equipment – a chandlery, to use the correct word – in a 1970s cinder-block structure. The store was in a minor industrial part of town, doomed to be gentrified in a few years; already the artists are starting to invade. Allison's daughter turned off the ignition, got out, stood up, and looked at me from behind her car. I was in the alley, and I turned off my engine and sat there and looked back at her, making eye contact across the cars and asphalt. Jason once told me that eye contact is the most intimacy two people can have – forget sex – because the optic nerve is technically an extension of the brain, and when two people look into each other's eyes, it's brain-to-brain. Having said that: if I had had a gun – I don't know – maybe I'd have popped her.

So the moment had arrived. She kept staring at me, and then she closed her car door and came over. "She's been lying to you," she said.

I didn't know what to reply.

"She's been feeding you a line."

What could I say?

"My name is Jessica. I know what you're here for. I can give it to you."

Her tone of voice told me that what she had to tell me was neither what I'd expected, nor what I wanted to hear. I was a defeated woman, and she knew it. She held out an arm to me, and I came to it as I might have come to that light you're supposed to see once you die.

"Have a seat. Here. Beside the planter." She motioned me to sit down on a concrete planter that had been poured decades ago and was now crumbling like angry gray sugar. I sat, and she pulled some cigarettes out of her purse. "Do you want one?"

Part of the terror of being told something you know will shock you is that it takes you back to the time in your life when everything really was shocking; for me that was maybe age thirteen, when I was essentially friendless, and being told by my mother that I'd one day blossom. I remember wanting peers; I remember wanting people in my life who could help me make all the fun mistakes. Crime? Maybe that's why I'm a stenographer. I hesitated and then said yes, I'd like a cigarette.

"You don't smoke, do you?"

"This is the second time this week I've had something resembling this conversation. Yes, I want a cigarette. I suppose, yes, I do smoke now."

She gave me one and lit it with her lighter and then lit her own. She said, "Mom's been telling you some pretty wild stuff, huh?"

"She has." I took a drag and I got dizzy, but I didn't mind. I wanted this experience to have a biological component to intensify it.

"It's not what you think it is."

"I started guessing as much last night."

"You think I slept with your boyfriend, don't you?"

I put the cigarette down on the concrete. "I did."

"When did you stop thinking that?"

"A minute ago. When you got out of your car and looked at me across the alley over there. You have a clear conscience."

"I'm sorry I have to tell you what I'm going to tell you. I can shut up if you like."

"No. Don't. I deserve whatever you're going to say."

Two crows landed on the pavement across the street and began cawing wildly at each other. There were needles and condoms on the alley's paving; late at night, this was the sex trade part of town. Jessica put her hand on my forearm. "No one deserves this. Heather, here's the deal: your boyfriend came to my mother about a year ago. He brought this sheet of paper with him. He gave my mom five hundred bucks and told her that if he ever went missing, then she should contact you and tell you these things as if he'd spoken to you from the dead – or from wherever it is he's gone to. He wanted you to be happy."

I sucked in air as if punched. It's the only way to describe it.

"And so my mom did that with you – she saw the story in the *North Shore News* that he had gone missing – "

"Jason. His name was Jason."

"Sorry. That *Jason* had gone missing. She called me at work yesterday and told me what she was up to, and I drove to her place and really lashed into her."

I'd seen the fight. I trusted this woman.

"My mom told me how she wasn't answering your calls. She has call display and can count every time you phoned. She's sneaky. She knew exactly what she was doing. She was milking you. And she was going to milk you dry. She has you pegged for another ten grand."

I stared at the ground. Jessica said, "Smoke your cigarette."

So we sat there and smoked. Her coworkers filed in, and she waved to them, and there was nothing really out of the ordinary about two women smoking together outside a workplace on a cold clear Canadian October day in the year 2002.

"What did Jason ever get into that'd make him think he might disappear some day?"

"I don't know."

* * *

Five years ago, before I met Jason, I had a depression or whatever you want to call it, and one morning I felt so dead I called Larry and pleaded bubonic plague. He had seen the clouds accumulating inside me and told me to phone the doctor; bless him, I did. At first they tried out some of the more fashionable antidepressants on me. They either nauseated me or made me buzzy and I had to say no to maybe six of them. There was one, the sixth one – I forget the name – which did this odd thing to me. I took it in the morning, and around lunch I had this impulse to kill myself. I don't mean to shock here; what I'm saying is that people talk about killing themselves all the time, and some people give it a go, and I'd always known that, but this pill, it opened up a door inside me: for the first time ever I actually understood how it *felt* to want to kill myself.

The drug wore off quickly, and the next prescription did the trick. After about three months I was my usual self again, and stopped taking anything.

The point here is that there are certain human behavioral traits that can be talked about, but unless you've experienced the impulse behind them, they remain theoretical. Most of the time, this is for the best. After my brush with the suicidal impulse, I listen with new ears to others when they speak on the subject. I think there are people who were born with that little door open, and they have to go through life knowing that they might jump through it at any moment.

In a similar vein, I think there is the impulse to be violent. When Jason and I fought, I'd be so angry that my eyeballs scrunched up and I saw black-and-white geometric patterns inside my head, but never, ever, would I consider hitting him, and Jason was the same way. We spoke about this once during a lunch down by the ocean – about anger and violence – and he said that no matter how angry he ever became with me, violence wasn't an option for him; it didn't even occur to him. He confided that there were *other* situations where violence was an option for him – obviously,

the Delbrook Massacre, but who knows what else? I suppose I'll go to the grave wondering what they were – but
with me? No.

Why am I saying this? Because Jason simply didn't have
the suicide impulse, nor do I think he was a violent guy. So I
don't worry that he jumped from a bridge or got killed in
some fight.

I should add, that when Jason and I fought, the characters
went away. To have dragged our characters into a fight
simply wasn't a possibility, any more than suicide or hitting
each other. Our characters were immune to the badness in
the world, a trait that made them slightly holy. As we didn't
have children, they became our children. I worried about
them the same way I worry about Barb's kids. I'll be having
my day, walking around the dog run down at Ambleside,
say, and then suddenly, *pow!* my stomach turns to a pile of
bricks, and I nearly collapse with anticipatory grief as I
realize the boys could burn themselves or be kidnapped or be
in a car accident. Or I'll be near tears when I think of
Froggles alone by himself in an apartment with nobody to
phone, no food in the fridge, maybe drinking some leftover
Canadian Club, wondering why we even bother going on
with our lives. Or I worry about Bonnie the Lamb, recently
shorn, lost from the flock, cold and sick with loneliness on
the wrong side of a raging river. I probably don't have to say
much more on this subject.

And then there is me, sad little me, living in a dream,
staring out the window, never again to find love. With Jason
I thought I'd finally played my cards right, and now I'm just
one more of those broken, sad people out there, figuring out
a year in advance where they can have Easter and Christmas

dinner without feeling like a burden or duty to others, cursing the quality of modern movies because it's so hard to fill weeknights with movies when they're all crap, and waiting, just waiting, for those three drinks a night to turn into four – and then, well, then I'll be applying my makeup in the morning, combing my hair, washing my clothes, but it's not really *for* anyone. I'm alive, but so what.

*   *   *

After my cigarette with Jessica I drove back to Lynn Valley, up to Allison's house. I know her real name is Cecilia, but she remains Allison to me.

Her Cutlass was in the carport. The newspapers were still on the front doormat, so I picked them up and rang the bell. Through the badly built 1960s contractor door, I heard shuffling up the stairs from where I knew the kitchen was. There were three glass slits in the door, and I looked through them and saw Allison, who stopped on the third step up, looked at me, and froze. It took her maybe half a minute to thaw out, and she came to the door and opened it, a tiny brass security chain across the gap.

"Heather. It's awfully early."

"I know it is." She'd have to be a moron not to see a certain level of madness in my eye, but I could tell she misread this as desperation for a message from Jason.

"I suppose I could let you in."

"Please do."

She unclasped the chain and said to come upstairs to the kitchen for coffee. "You look terrible," she said, "like you didn't sleep last night."

"I didn't."

The kitchen was generic North Van – lemon-lime freckled

linoleum floor with four decades of wear patterns showing, SPCA fridge magnets, vitamins on the windowsill, and through that window, the primordial evergreen maw that continues from Lynn Valley until the end of the world. She said, "I know it must be troubling to wait for messages to come in from loved ones."

I said, "I'm not even going to dignify that with a response."

She looked at me and at my small insurrection. "Heather, I do the best I can." She handed me a coffee, and I sat and stared at her. She had to be an incredible dolt not to see trouble lurking. "Last night was psychically very active, and I think I received something you might be interested in."

I smiled.

"Again, it's something that makes no sense to me, but these words do seem to mean something important to you."

"How much will they cost me?"

"Heather! No need to be so crass."

"I'm out of money. Yesterday was it."

Allison didn't like this. "Oh, really?"

"I don't know what to do."

"I'm a businesswoman, Heather. I can't just do these things for free."

"I can see not."

I sipped the coffee, too hot and too weak. I placed the mug on the tabletop and looked at my hands. Allison watched me. I began tugging away at a diamond ring on my left ring finger, a diamond the size of a ladybug. Sometimes with Jason, subjects were best left undiscussed. I'd always assumed the ring had fallen off the back of a truck, but then

Barb told me she'd actually gone with Jason to Zales to help select it. "I have this ring."

Allison came over and, with the deadened eyes of a Soviet flea marketeer, appraised it in a blink. "I suppose so."

The ring came free. I handed it to her, and as she reached for it, I grabbed her, yanked her forward and with my right arm put her in a headlock. I said, "Look, you scheming cow. Your daughter filled me in on your little prank here, and if you want to live past lunchtime, you take me to wherever you keep the sheet of paper Jason gave you, and you hand it over. Got it?"

"Let go of me."

I turned her around and dug a knee into her back. I've never struck another human being before, but I had size on my side. "Don't screw with me. I've got a brown belt in Tae Bo. I studied down in Oregon. So where is it?"

"I can't . . . *breathe*."

I loosened my grip. "You bring tears to my eyes. Come on. Where is it?"

"Downstairs."

"So that's where we'll go."

I felt like I'd been given a prescription drug that opened a fifty-pound pair of oak double doors, doors I'd somehow overlooked before. To be even clearer, I felt like a man. It was surprisingly easy taking full control of Allison's body, but I don't think I'd have killed her. Whatever door this new door was, it wasn't the murder door.

The stairs were tricky but doable. We entered a room that must once have been Glenn's office but had, over the years, been converted to a transient storage area for bankers' boxes full of old books and papers. A sun-bleached litho of mallard ducks in flight had been removed from over the desk and leaned against the floor below, leaving a ghostly rectangle on the wall. Straddling this ghost was a brass-framed piece of fuzzily photographed flowers embossed with some sort of poetic nonsense in that casual fake-handwriting font people use on invitations to their second and third marriages. Allison's feminizing touch. The room had an aura of bankruptcy and defeat.

"Where is it?"

"In the middle drawer."

"Let's go fetch it then, shall we?"

We approached the desk with the gracelessness of captor and captive. I allowed her just enough mobility to open the drawer, and once it was open, I yanked back her arm and said, "Let me do a quick inspection here for guns and knives." I mussed through the desk's contents and then I saw Jason's handwriting on some sheets of crumpled pink invoice paper from his boss's contracting firm. On seeing it, I squeaked and let go of Allison and picked it up and held it to my chest. She fell to the floor, was about to rise, and then ended up just slumping against a bookcase. She said, "I suppose you're – "

"Oh, shut up." I looked at the paper and Jason's little-boy printing. His writing was small and efficient, and he managed to cram a lot onto the pages. There were dozens of our characters and their best-known exploits, along with staging instructions:

Froggles is the most *important* and beloved character. He speaks in a high voice, but if you tell him he sounds shrill, he indignantly shrieks, "I'm not *shrill!*" He drives a Dodge Scamp he bought at a garage sale. Primary enjoyments include winning spelling bees, twelve-packs of crunchy flies and *Law & Order* reruns.

Bonnie T. Lamb is the crabbiest and most politically correct character. She wears an African beanie and horn-rimmed glasses, has a bleating voice and can easily have her opinion swayed by her personal kryptonite, Cloverines. Her other weaknesses include bad arts and crafts and working in B-movies as a walk-on. Her life partner, Cherish, fixes motorcycles.

And so forth. I sat down in Glenn's captain's chair and inhaled Jason's letter like it was cherry blossoms. Allison posed no threat. I'd just heard from the dead.

Allison said, "He's gone. You know it, right?"

"I know."

"I'm not trying to be a bitch here. But he's gone. Glenn went. He went and I was left behind. This big stupid house and me and nothing else, and our savings lost in some idiotic tech stock."

I looked at her.

"The only reason I became a psychic was to try and reach Glenn. I thought that maybe if I pretended to be one I could become one. The things I did to try to become one – diets, purges, fasts, seminars, weekends. All of it just pointless."

"You tried to rip me off."

"I did. But you know what? To have seen your face whenever I gave you some words – it was all I'd ever wanted for myself."

I was appalled. "How could you use extortion when you were doing something so . . . *sacred*?"

Allison turned toward me, amused that I didn't get her punch line: "Well, my dear, I'm broke. When you're my age, you'll understand."

She was still on the floor when I got up and left. I drove home and put Jason's list of instructions inside a jumbo freezer-size zip-top bag in order to protect his pencilings from rubbing away completely. I removed my shoes and belt and fell into bed, holding an edge of the bag up to my face, and sleep came easily.

Part Four

2003: Reg

Jason, my son, unlike you, I grew up amid the dank smothering alder leaves of Agassiz, far from the city. In summer I could tell you the date simply by chronicling the number of children who had drowned in the Fraser River or been poisoned by the laburnum pods that dangled from branches and so closely resembled runner beans. I spent those summer days on the Fraser's gravel bars, watching eagles in the tall snagged trees browse for salmon, but I wasn't in the river just for the scenery – it was piety. I believed the maxim that should I lose my footing, God would come in and carry me wherever the river was deepest. The water felt like an ongoing purification, and I've never felt as clean as I did then. That was so many decades ago – the Fraser is now probably full of fish rendered blind by silt from gravel quarries, its surface pocked with bodies that somehow worked themselves loose from their cement kimonos.

Autumn? Autumn was a time of sorting out the daffodil bulbs with their malathion stink, brushing their onionskin coatings from overly thick sweaters knit by two grandmothers who refused to speak English while they carded wool. Winters were spent in the rain, grooming the fields – I was raised to believe that the opposite of labor is theft, not leisure. I remember my boots sinking in mud that tried to steal my knees, its sucking noise. And then there was spring – always the spring – when the mess and stink and garbage of the rest of the year were redeemed by the arrival of the flowers. I was so proud of them – proud, me . . . Reginald Klaasen – proud that they loaned innocence and beauty to a land that was never really tamed. Proud from walking in the fields, inside the yellow that smelled of birth and forgiveness – only to stare north, out at the forest and its black green clutch, always taunting me, inviting me inside, away from the sun. Hiding something – but what?

Perhaps hiding the Sasquatch. The legend of the Sasquatch has always been potent in my mind – the man-beast who supposedly lives in the tree-tangled forests. It was the Sasquatch I'd always identified with, and perhaps you can see why: a creature lost in the wilderness, forever in hiding, seeking companionship and friendship, living alone, without words or kindness from others. How I hoped to find the Sasquatch – hoped to bring him out of the forest and into the world! I planned to teach him words and clothe him and save him in as many ways as I could. My mother encouraged me to do this, to save the soul of this damned beast, bear witness to him, make him one of us, force him to gain a world while surrendering his mystery. I sometimes wondered whether gaining the world and losing one's mystery was such a good deal, and I felt ashamed of thinking this. The world is a good place, rain and mud and man-eating forests included. God created the world – I believe that. No theory of creation satisfies me, but I have this sureness in my heart.

I remember finding out that the world was actually just a planet, in school in the third grade, and I remember hating the teacher, Mr. Rowan, who discussed the solar system as if it were a rock collection. It's so hard to balance in our minds the knowledge that "the world" is, mundanely, "a planet." The former is so holy; the latter merely a science project. I walked out of class, indignant, and spent a week at home as the school and my father tried to negotiate a meeting point between the rock-collection creation theory of the earth and the more decent and spiritual notion of "the world." None was reached. I was put in another teacher's class.

My father was an angry man, you know that, but he was also a man of little faith, constantly angry because – because why? Because he took over his father's daffodil farm and forfeited whatever life he might have created for himself. My father was fierce, and I was fierce with you, Jason, and when I became fierce with you, I was appalled yet unable to stop myself.

My fierceness with you came not from any desire to copy my father, but instead from my desire to be his opposite, to be righteous, and to be strong where my own father was weak. My piety galled him, and when he was furious, I was driven out of the house and fields with threats of the leather strap he used for sharpening his razor, out into the forest, away from home, for hours, sometimes days (yes, I ran away from home) spent contemplating a God who would create an animal like my father, a religious man without faith. A fake man – a human form containing nothing.

I never told you about my childhood. Why would I have? I

told Kent, but never you. I suppose I thought you'd twist the words and use them against me. You never said much around the house, but you were a formidable opponent. I could see it in your eyes when you were a year old. You were *competition*. Children are cruel in their ability to instantly identify a fraud, and that, especially, was your gift and curse. I was so insecure about my beliefs that I feared being exposed by my own child. That was wretched of me.

Your childhood: as an infant you were a crier, a creature of colicky squalls that frightened your mother and me until we went to a doctor and he asked some questions and it turned out that the only time you ever cried was just before or after sleeping – that technically you were asleep, sleep-walking, and what we were seeing was your interior life – screaming in your dreams! Good Lord! As the years wore on, we thought you were mute, or possibly autistic; you didn't start speaking until you were four. That is family legend. Your first words weren't "Mama" or "Dada," but rather, "Go away." Your mother was devastated, whereas I heard your words only as a challenge to my authority.

Listen to me, already – the words of a lonely broken man in his little apartment somewhere on the edge of the New World. Let me change tactics. Maybe I can see myself better that way . . .

Here:

Reg, always thought that God had a startling revelation to hand him, a divine mission; that's why he always seemed so aloof and arrogant and distant from the people and events around him: he was the chosen one. And of course, Reg's mission never came. Instead, he was in his lunchroom one afternoon, eating an egg salad sandwich, when his secretary burst in and said there was a shooting at his son's high school. This father of two drove across town, listening to the AM radio news, which only got worse and worse, and the world became more dreamlike and unreal to him. Reg hadn't even crossed the Lions Gate Bridge yet, and newscasters were already counting the dead. And here is where Reg's great crime began: he was jealous that God had given a mission not to him, but to his son. To his son, I might add, who was, according to the several Spanish Inquisition members of his youth group, having intimate relations with a young woman in his class. Jason's relations with Cheryl were, to the mind of a smug and wrongly righteous man, like lemon juice on a stove burn. Of course, in Reg's mind his son's crime wasn't as clearly defined as this. That sort of clarity comes only with decades. Instead, he was simply furious with heaven and God and had no idea why. So once home, in a flash he seized upon his son's act of bravery as an act of cowardice and the devil. He held a two-second-long kangaroo court inside his head, and rejected his son.

When Reg's wife heard this and crippled him using a lamp powered by an astonishingly hard blast to his knee, he was confused and had no idea why the world had turned on him. But it was the other way around – Reg was in La-La Land. He was expelled from his own home, where even he knew he was no longer master. In the hospital, nobody, save for his firstborn son, visited him – why would anybody want to visit such a miscreant? The only other exception was the complaining and hostile wraith that his sister had become, who drove in once a week from Agassiz. She demanded gas money and shamed Reg by pointing out how few flowers he'd been sent in the hospital – only some limp gladioli in yellow water, supplied by his office.

When Reg was released from the hospital, he moved into a new apartment in a new building owned by his boss's brother-in-law. He went back to work, but no one spoke to him much – there were condolences and expressions of gladness that Jason had been exonerated, but his coworkers knew he'd been abandoned by his family, that he lived alone, and that this was all, somehow, connected to his pride and his vanity.

Vanity.

When Reg was courting his wife-to-be, he thought he should spiff himself up a bit, so, being frugal but optimistic, he went to Value Village, a former grocery store now filled with mildewed socks and blouses and plastic kitchenware. He found a pair of mint condition – *unworn!* – black shoes in his size for a dollar forty-nine. *Whooee!* He was so proud of those shoes, and he wore them out of the store, into the rain where he was to meet his gal, just getting off her shift at Nuffy's Donuts. He walked into the donut shop, where even ugly yellow fluorescent tubes couldn't diminish her complexion. She was putting a jacket over her work uniform. She looked down and said, "What the *jeez* happened to your feet?" His feet had turned into bundles of soggy paper. The shoes he'd purchased were mortuary shoes, designed only for open coffins, never to be worn by the living. Cheapness and vanity.

Your mother.

She's technically alive, but she isn't really here, she is far gone in her alcoholic dementia, her liver on its final boozy gasp. I take the blame – I liked her drunk, because she was a quiet and amiable drunk. When she was drunk, her eyes lost that accusatory look. When she was drunk, she gave the impression she'd ride life unchanged right through to the end, that her life was spiritually adequate, that she wore a crown of stars. This drunken look absolved me of all the guilt I felt regarding the slow-motion demolition of the once pretty girl who always saved two Boston creme donuts for me, and who unashamedly loved color TV, and who (and this is the hard part) seemed spiritual in a way that didn't make me want to preach to her. She could have married any man she wanted, but she chose *Reg Klaasen*. . . . Why? Because she thought I was spiritual, too. I don't know when it dawned on her that I wasn't, that I was merely someone whose vocabulary was slightly old-fashioned, and whose ideas were stolen almost entirely from dead people. I suppose that would be when she started drinking, just after you were born and she had a hysterectomy. It must have been devastating to her, to realize she'd hitched herself to a religious fraud. And I led her on – that's my own disgrace. And now her life's basically over. I visit her twice a month at the facility near Mount Seymour Parkway. The first time I went there I was unsure whether I should go. I was convinced she'd throw an IV-tree at me, or go into hysterics like Elizabeth Taylor in *Suddenly, Last Summer,* but instead she smiled and said she had some donuts tucked away for me, and then she kept on saying it, with no OFF switch, and that was the worst rebuke of all.

Kent.

When Kent died, I found that physically leaving earth was a desirable notion. I was at work when I learned of his death, out by the front reception area trying to unjam a roll of fax paper. I was irritated and I'd told the receptionist to put me on speakerphone, and that's where I was when Barb's mother told me. I fell to my knees and I saw a wash of light, and then I saw a fleet of dazzling metal spaceships, like bullets aimed at the sun, and I wanted to walk toward them and get inside one, and leave everything behind. And then the everyday world returned. I'd had that vision, the only vision I've ever had, but it told me nothing and offered no comfort. So, what good was that? And what was left in my life? At the funeral you shunned me, as did your mother. I can't say I blame you. My family in the Valley? They're junkyard dogs now, what's left of them. And then last year you vanished, and all that remains are the twins – the spitting image of you, I might add. And there's Barb, grudgingly, and (I'm not stupid) only at the behest of Heather. Heather is a fine woman, a woman you're so lucky to have had enter your life: a heart as big as the Hoover Dam, and a soul as clear as ice cubes.

I sound maudlin here. I don't want that. I'm not striving for effect, and I'm not drunk. But to spit things out in a list like this is humbling. Lists only spell out the things that can be taken away from us by moths and rust and thieves. If something is valuable, don't put it in a list. Don't even say the words.

Ruth.

There. And she's gone, too. She was the trumpet that returned me from the dead. I know you must have seen her photo that day when you came to fetch things at my apartment – you never missed a trick of mine. So you know what she looked like, large but not fat – you'd never describe her as plump – with hair the color of rich soil and – Cripes, listen to me discuss this woman like a 4-H Club sow.

By the time you saw her photo we'd been dating – what a silly word – for years. We met at an insurance seminar downtown, where she gave a short speech on insuring the elderly, and I liked her because she had a sense of humor in the face of that day's technical blathering. I also learned from her that I have a hint of a sense of humor myself. Yes, I can already see your face puckering with disbelief. So be it.

I lost Ruth for two reasons, the first of which was the seed of the second: I didn't want to take her to Kent's funeral; why, I don't know. I could plead crazed grief, but even still. She said I was ashamed because I was still married to your mother, and that I had a schoolboy's shame that people would stare at us and imagine the two of us making love out of wedlock. How pathetic. And she was right. Ruth was always right. But she was a deep believer, too, and willing to endure my crotchety trespasses.

When you went missing, I fell apart, although I doubt you'll believe that. Two sons gone – how is a man supposed to feel? Ruth was a help at first, but then she learned I was still going to visit your mother twice a month, and she told me it was time I divorced your mother and married her. I ought to have hired a skywriting jet to say YES. But no. I said that marriage was until death – this from a man who went for a decade not communicating with his wife. Such a hypocrite.

We were in the Keg at the foot of Lonsdale when she told me her stance, and I told her of my counter-decision. For the first time since I'd known her, she froze me out. For Kent's funeral she'd showed me forgiveness, but that night in the restaurant? She went crazy with a calm face, justifiably so. We'd shared so much, and to have our bank of memories turned against me? Ruth had no idea that even though I was sitting there with zucchini sticks and dipping sauce in front of me, blinking my eyes, in my mind I was already dead, and I was standing at the gates of heaven, the way I'd always imagined the first part of death to be like, being shown a film clip version of my life – a naïve vision, but one common to men of my age. Even after all I'd been through, I'd still assumed I'd sail through those gates; such presumption is itself a sin. But as Ruth listed smaller reasons for leaving me, I knew I was further away from the gates than I'd ever dreamed. I had always believed I'd been leading an upstanding life, immune to all forms of interrogation, but among other things, Ruth told me I thought like an infant, that I was confusing what I thought was right with what God thought was right, and that I was harder to please than God, and who exactly did I think I was? And then she told me that she was leaving, and that once she was out the door I would never be loved by anybody ever again, and that I'd brought all of this upon myself.

Have you ever known what it's like to be loved by nobody? Maybe you have, but no, that's not possible, because your mother never failed you. Me? I didn't know what to do – I was shattered, and in a moment of weakness I phoned your Heather. I arrogantly assumed that because her family all lived far away, she must feel equally unloved from her side – and in this I was correct, *but* she said I didn't have to feel guilty for calling her for that reason.

It's strange, but once you begin to confess your weaknesses, one confession leads to another, and the effect is astonishingly liberating. At my age, it was a little like having food poisoning – all that bile and poison sprayed out of me in every direction – a process that took a few weeks as Heather and I tried to find you. It wasn't until I felt emptied of lies and weaknesses that, as with recovering from a poisoning, I felt mending begin.

Heather.

I want to discuss that false psychic you paid to bring Heather messages from the dead. It was a thoughtful idea, but one that backfired and then, ultimately, in its own way, frontfired, giving Heather more hope than you'd imagine. But, Lord Almighty, did that psychic woman pull a number on Heather! Right from the get-go she began extorting money – thousands. People like that woman make it clear just how asinine it is to believe that human beings have some kind of built-in universal sense of goodness. These days I think that everybody's just one spit away from being a mall bomber. People say sugary nice things all the time, but believe none of it. See how many weapons people have stockpiled; inspect their ammo cache; read their criminal records; get them drunk and bring up God; and then you *really* know what it is you have to protect yourself from. Forget intentions – learn the deeds of which they're capable.

Anyway, in the end, Heather twigged onto this psychic's game plan. In doing so she told me about your characters; I had no idea you had this other world inside your head, and if you ever read these words, I imagine you'll blush as you do so, but don't. Froggles! Bonnie! Gerard! The characters are pure delight – they're lime sherbet and maraschino cherries – they're almost holy. Your characters – *that* was the sort of thing I ought to have been telling you at bedtime rather than squeezing out of you your daily list of trespasses. God, I was a grim old sucker. Just so you know, Heather quit her job at the courts, and she's now working full-time making children's books using your characters. They're good little books, and one might even be published locally. Heather and Barb allow me to read them to the twins, so I come out of this a winner. And again, I have to say how much the twins resemble you. I wonder what Kent would have thought? He's fading from my memory, you know. Sometimes I have to work to conjure up his face or his voice. I oughtn't be telling you that, because it means that I'll forget your face and voice someday, too. (But don't take it that way.)

I'm in a Kinko's writing this. I haven't said that yet. It's downtown and open twenty-four hours. It's maybe one A.M. and I'm the only customer here on this side of the store. Two other people – homesick German tourists, I'm guessing – are across the room trying to send a fax.

I think heaven must be a little bit like this place – everybody with a purpose, in a beautiful clean environment. They even have those wonderful new full-spectrum lights that make you look like you've just returned from a stroll in an Irish mist.

Why am I here? I'm here because I still don't have a computer, and I'm here writing this because today I got a call from the RCMP out in Chilliwack. They called to say that they'd found your "highly weathered" flannel shirt, and in its pocket, your Scotiabank debit card. It was tangled in some bulrushes in a swamp beside a forest out there, found by some kids shooting BB guns. I asked the RCMP if they were going to organize a manhunt, and while they didn't laugh aloud, they made it clear that one was not being planned. How dare they. All they gave me was a map.

And so I'm typing this letter out. I'm going to print it and make a thousand copies, and come sunrise I'm going to go out to that swamp and its surrounding forest and I'm going to tack these letters onto the trees there with a pack of brightly colored tacks I saw up by the front desk when I registered to use this machine.

I know that kind of forest so well, and at this time of year, too: spiderwebs vacant, their builders snug inside cocoons; sumac and vine maples turned yellow and red, smelling like chilled candy. The hemlocks and firs and cedars, evergreen but also everdark. The way sounds turn into shadows, and how easy it is to stay hidden forever should that be your wish. You're the Sasquatch now, searching for someone to take away your loneliness, dying as you live with your sense of failed communion with others. You're hidden but you're there, Jason. And I clearly remember from when I was growing up, the Sasquatch was never without hope, even if all he had to be hopeful about was bumping into me one day. But isn't that something?

You might ask me whether I still believe in God; I do – and maybe not even in the best sense of the word "believe." In the end, it might boil down to some sort of insurance equation to the effect that it's three percent easier to believe than not to believe. Is that cynical? I hope not. I may sell insurance, but I grieve, I accept. I rebel. I submit. And then I repeat the cycle. I doubt I can ever believe with the purity of heart your Cheryl once had.

Cheryl.

We never once spoke about her. We never even spoke, period. I never told you that her mother phoned me about eight years ago – I'm listed in the book – and she said that until that day she'd always believed you were involved in the shootings, but then, "It's the funniest thing. I was making coffee this morning, I went to put an extra apple in Lloyd's attaché case, because the apples are so good this time of year, and inside his case, between two folders was a paperback about the massacre, and it was open to the page with Jason's photo – I hadn't seen that image in years. I don't know why, but I finally realized Jason was innocent." Stupid, stupid woman, but a woman whose daughter was lost in the worst imaginable way. As you were never a father, you can never imagine what it is to lose your child. That's not a challenge – how grotesque if it were. It's a simple statement of fact.

But I haven't lost you, my son. No no no. And you *will* find one of these letters. I know you will. You never missed a trick of mine, so why stop now? And when you do find this letter, you know what? Something extraordinary will happen. It will be like a reverse solar eclipse – the sun will start shining down in the middle of night, imagine that! – and when I see this sunlight it will be my signal to go running out into the streets, and I'll shout over and over, "Awake! Awake! The son of mine who once was lost has now been found!" I'll pound on every door in the city, and my cry will ring true: "Awake! Everyone listen, there has been a miracle – my son who once was dead is now alive. Rejoice! All of you! Rejoice! You must! My son is coming home!"

A Note on the Author

Douglas Coupland is the author of the novels *Generation X, Miss Wyoming,* and most recently *All Families Are Psychotic,* among others, as well as the nonfiction works *Polaroids from the Dead, City of Glass,* and *Souvenir of Canada.* He grew up and lives in Vancouver.

A Note on the Type

The text of this book is set in Linotype Sabon, named after the type founder, Jacques Sabon. It was designed by Jan Tschichold and jointly developed by Linotype, Monotype, and Stempel, in response to a need for a typeface to be available in identical form for mechanical hot metal composition and hand composition using foundry type.

Tschichold based his design for Sabon roman on a fount engraved by Garamond, and Sabon italic on a fount by Granjon. It was first used in 1966 and has proved an enduring modern classic.